TRUST ME

CINDI PAGE

 PAGE ONE
PUBLISHING

Lest we forget.

For Lesley, who knew how to get creative with army rations.

ONE

ADAM

Evie Simpson is impossible to defuse.

I've lost count of how many bombs I've pulled apart in my career, yet, here I am, unable to defuse this situation with Evie. It's life or death, just like in the field, but I can't seem to find a detonator switch when I'm standing here watching the only woman, who's ever truly loved me, throw my clothes into an empty suitcase. She's crying —no sobbing—and she's yelling louder than I knew she ever could. And just like when I'm in a hotspot, I don't move, trying to make sense of what's going on around me.

It's all happening in slow motion. I'm watching my civilian clothes, the ones she has picked for me, fly through the air like debris, most of them missing the open suitcase. Just my luck, a checkered shirt I have no love for seems to be the only bloody thing to land in the bag. I run my fingers through my hair which is already clipped short for my deployment. I can feel despair camouflaged as

1

anger take up arms in me, and I have to make every effort to keep my mouth shut and not explode, as well.

She's heaving now, out of breath from the exertion of pulling clothes off hangers just out of her reach and throwing them as hard as she can. Her dark red hair is wilder than I've seen it in years. She has stopped shouting and is standing dangerously still, staring at me. The hard, dull look in her eyes tells me that a cockroach might have more status in her world than I do right now. She never used to look at me this way. There was a time when I saw myself through her eyes; I knew I was her everything and she mine.

"Are you just going to stand there? Say something!" Her words come out like a hiss.

"What do you want me to say? That your tantrum worked and I'll stay?"

She stares me down, arms crossed over her chest, eyes narrow. I know that's exactly what she wants—for me to quit the army once and for all.

"I can't do that. I'm a—"

She cuts me off. "Spare me 'I'm a soldier' speech, Adam. I've heard it too many times. No matter how dangerous the deployment is, how many times we've had to put off starting a life together properly, you always choose fighting other people's wars over me."

"That's not true."

"It is! It's exactly what you're doing right now. Again."

"I'm going to work, for God's sake, not abandoning you. Why can't you see it that way?"

"Afghanistan is not 'work', it's a war zone. It's only

going to work when you actually come home afterwards —and that's not something you can guarantee, is it?"

I could not answer her. She was right. I could not promise her that I would come home uninjured, dead, or at all.

"I've been training for this my whole life. And they're letting me lead my own team, Evie. Don't you understand how important this is to me?"

I watched the emotion on her face from moments before evaporate in a second, leaving her expression harder than stone.

"I've waited thirteen years, Adam. I've waited for you to do your thing in the army. And here we are. I'll turn thirty while you're on tour. Do you know what that means?"

I did. She wants to start a family...but the time has never seemed right.

Has never seemed right to me.

I don't say anything.

"You can pretend like we have all the time in the world. And as a guy, I guess that's true for you. But not for me. I don't want to be an old mum. And you know that. You've known it forever."

I did.

"And what if I was pregnant? What would you do then?"

"Are you?"

"No!"

She's exasperated again. "You're missing the point."

Somewhere in the lull of the angry outbursts, sadness has crept into her voice. I don't just hear it, I feel

3

it, and it's like the blade of a knife being pushed into my chest.

"Six months, Evie. Please. Please...wait for me." I'm breaking.

"It's not just six months, Adam, is it? It's another six months on top of the last thirteen years we can never have back."

"But when I get back—"

"Stop. No."

"Evie," I say her name like a cry for help.

I watch her squeeze her eyes shut so hard that fresh tears fall over her blotchy cheeks. Over the years, her freckles have faded; sometimes I miss them. When she opens her eyes, she doesn't look at me and she takes long strides towards the door.

I step in the path and block her as she reaches the door. One year, for Valentine's Day, I painted the door fire-engine red. It's her favourite colour. She adored my present, even though it cost nothing more than a tenner and my time. And I loved her for that.

"Please." It's the only word I can muster.

She looks up at me. Her green, gold-flecked eyes are bright with tears. "Will you stay?"

For a million reasons I can't explain to her, I can't give her what she wants today. I need this opportunity to prove myself.

"I didn't think so."

I let her pass. I hear her cry as she picks up her handbag and keys. She pauses as she turns the brass door-knob and looks back at me. I've followed her like a latent shadow. Silent. Dumbstruck.

"Goodbye, Adam. I wish I could be what you need. Be the girl that waits. I just can't anymore. I have no more wait left in me."

"But I love you, Evie."

She nods while more tears fall. And leaves anyway.

BOOM.

I'm dead.

I ARRIVE AT THE OFFICERS' mess with my poorly packed suitcase. It was understood between Evie and I that I would be the one to move out because we live in her house. Most soldiers live in accommodation provided by the army, clusters of cookie-cutter houses near the base. But because Evie is an only child, her parents gifted her the cash from a savings policy they set up before she was even born, and she used it for a deposit on the semi we've called home for the last nine years. I don't think women think about how much being a provider is wired into a man's DNA and how small we feel when that's taken away from us.

I turn the key in the lock to the seven-by-six room, and before I even step inside, I'm assaulted with the stench: a mix of damp and piss. I open the single window to let the air in. The metal cot and its standard six-inch foam mattress promise a chronic crick in the neck. I try not to linger on the fact that's where I'm at in my life. *Fucking hell.* I toss the bag and head straight out to find a scrubbing brush and disinfectant. There's no way I'm brushing my teeth over a basin that's doubled up as a urinal in a not-so-distant past life.

I spend an hour scrubbing down the room until everything smells of bleach. I make my bed and unpack my bag before I head down to the officers' cafeteria for some grub.

"Dickens!" Pete greets me as I carry my plate towards his table.

"Hey, mate." I greet him first and then reach to pat Foster's, our team's sniffer dog, on the head. She immediately leans in for more attention and I scratch her behind both ears.

"So you're here now?"

Pete has been my number two for the longest time and he is also Foster's handler. We did basic training together, and he's the one who christened me 'Dickens' because I carry an old and well-thumbed copy of *Great Expectations* with me. He knows the story with Evie, and I'm grateful that I don't have to find the words to speak of what a mess my life is just yet.

I nod, and he lets out a low whistle and shakes his head. "It's a real shame, mate. I thought you two were perfect together, but I guess both need to be willing to make sacrifices for it to work proper like."

I shove a fork full of dry, stringy chicken in my mouth and look away.

"I've been watching this show on Netflix." Pete changes the subject.

"Yeah?"

"How to live mortgage-free."

I laugh. Typical Pete. Always a scheme up his sleeve.

"Yeah? How do you do that on an army wage? Rob a bank?"

Pete shakes his head. "No, you just get really creative. One guy bought a double-decker bus and converted the whole fing for 25K!"

"So now he lives in a bus?"

"No, it's his house now, innit? And he can drive it and park it anywhere!"

"Not anywhere."

"Fair enough, but there are plenty of places he could get a permit for. It was really cool. Another woman and her husband converted a barge, and they dock in London! Imagine living in London, mate—and not paying rent, making some other dude rich."

"Uh-ha."

"Just watch the show." Pete's disappointment in my lack of enthusiasm pulls the corners of his mouth into a straight line.

"I'll watch it," I say to make him feel better.

After the passable supper, Pete tries to lure me to the local pub for a pint, but I'm not up for it, and it's cool of him to make us his special coffee instead. It's a slow-drip Vietnamese roast over a couple of shots of condensed milk. It's so sweet the spoon stands upright in the cup, but since I know I'll lose a stone or more, at least, while in Afghan, I ignore the trillion grams of sugar I'm about to consume. I end up sitting through an episode of *The Mortgage-Free Life* with him, both of us hunched over his phone in the rec room.

As much as I was to take the piss out of Pete for being

into this, I find myself googling properties under £10 000 during the show.

"Told ya." He shoulders me, his smile all teeth. All perfectly white and straight. It would annoy me that Pete is fit, but it's hard not to like the guy. He grew up almost worse than I did, and yet he's always laughing and carries life light, seemingly without a care in the world.

I scroll through images of crumbling outbuildings, which would be a 'renovators dream', and sigh. And then a familiar over-run cottage, with half the roof gone, makes me stop and scroll back. I click on the image.

Nestled in a Herefordshire woodland, this generously sized cottage has the potential to be a private country escape. Foundations solid. Offers from £10 000. Call 01432 2455689.

I flip through the images and recognise every angle of the white-washed walls. It's the secret spot where Evie and I would meet after school. We'd sit with our backs leaned against the wall in a hidden corner and daydream about our future. Sometimes she'd help me with my homework even though I was two years ahead of her. A lot of the time, we'd fool around and see how far we could go with our clothes still on.

I swallowed hard as the memories of our elicit rendezvous catch me unawares.

"Did ya find something?" Pete looks over my shoulder.

I nod. "It's a place Evie and I used to hang out at after school."

"Oh yeah? How much is it?" He squints to find the

price and gives a low whistle. "Not bad, mate, that's a decent price. How much you got saved?"

I side-eye him. "More than that," I say. And it's a 100 percent true. With Evie paying only a small mortgage, thanks to her parent's deposit money, and me spending the same on the utilities every month, my expenses are low, and I've been saving up to give Evie the wedding and honeymoon of her dreams; plus I've been building up a buffer for when I leave the army.

"Right"—Pete chuckles—"dark-horse Dickens. But fink about it, mate, you spend ten grand on buying the prop'ty and another twenty fixing it up, and then it's yours—forever, and you don't owe no one nuffing."

"It'll take more than twenty grand to get it liveable." But in my head, I'm working out how far I can get with the cash I have. The idea of not being beholden to Evie's family for the roof over our head will go a long way in setting things right between us. She always downplayed her family money, but the more she got, the more I felt I owed. Her father never approved of me because I grew up, according to him, without any family values. He is right about that—the foster-care system taught me some hard lessons, all of them geared for survival and not much else.

"You can do some of the work yourself—that will save loads."

"Just because I can do a few carpentry bits, doesn't make me qualified to renovate a whole house." I'm shooting Pete down, but I can feel excitement and possibility start to bubble inside me.

"That's what YouTube is for, innit?"

"Maybe."

I'M LYING flat on my back, staring at the ceiling in the dark. I miss my bed and Evie in it. I miss how she'd often be the big spoon and cradle me, with her breath, soft and warm on the back of my neck. I rearrange the pillow, trying to dispel the thoughts of things I can't do anything about. I don't want to think about deploying with nothing to come home to. It's dangerous. So I tell myself I haven't lost Evie yet. We're just giving each other a bit of space. We'll figure this out; we always do.

As sleep finally sucks me in, I imagine the derelict cottage beautifully restored and Evie standing in its doorway, calling me in.

Evie

THE SILENCE, when I enter the house, is dense, and already I can feel that Adam has left. It's as if we've come full circle. I'm sure he doesn't remember that it was fourteen years ago today that we met. Me, fifteen and new to the school. Adam, two years older.

We moved to Herefordshire because my father had been promoted to Deputy Headteacher at a sought-after boarding school in the county. Part of the perks and allure for my parents was that their only daughter got to attend St George's College *gratis*.

But that's not where I ended up. To the deep regret

of my father and a decent dose of professional humiliation we never speak of in my family, I didn't fit in with the la-di-das of St George's. I finished my schooling at a neighbouring state school which I travelled to by bus when I didn't fancy the twenty-five-minute walk. Subjecting me to public transport for my daily commute was my father's version of tough love, and on the days that it rained, which was often, it was really he who seemed to be suffering instead of me. The bus meant time with Adam.

It was on my very first day at Greenthorne that I literally fell head over heels for a boy with jet-black hair and the bluest eyes I'd ever seen. He was marching with the army cadet group in the school quad; I later learned this was a practice for an upcoming parade. The squad had halted to attention and brought four fingers up to their foreheads in a salute. I was passing the practice on my way to the bus stop when I found myself rooted to the spot, watching the older boys in their green camo uniforms. My eyes soon spied the most handsome one of them all. He was tall, broad-shouldered, with a terrible buzz cut. He must have felt my eyes on him because I saw his jaw twitch. And then, without the green beret on his head moving an inch, his cobalt-blue eyes found mine. Thanks to my genetic predisposition, my face flushed from the jowls up to the root tips of my hair.

Jolted out of my daze, I made tracks to walk away as fast as I could. That should have been the end of it, but an uneven cement block tripped me up. It catapulted me forward. I cried out when my palms scraped the cruel concrete. Ambiguous tears, half mortification, half shame, followed. Not my finest moment.

"Are you okay?" He was picking up my rucksack and extending a hand to help me up.

"I'm fine," I sniffed, avoiding those intense cobalt eyes, and instead winced when I inspected my hands which were rubbed raw.

"You should get that cleaned up."

I dusted the grit off each hand the best I could. "I'm fine. I was just leaving."

"Wait." I watched him jog to the platoon leader, exchange a few words while looking back at me just once, before going to pick up his own bag.

"I'll walk with you. Where are you going?"

"Bus stop. I take the 436."

"Me too."

He was still carrying my bag. We walked away from the platoon leaders barking commands, and when we took the corner towards the road, he started talking.

"You're new here."

I nodded; apparently, I was mute.

"Do you have a name?" He cracked a cheeky grin that revealed a deep dimple on his left cheek. I tried to take a deep breath to calm the nervous excitement that seemed to have befallen me, but instead, I gulped at the air like a guppy and almost choked.

"Eve," I managed.

He stopped dead and cut me short. "Funny. Haha. Jesus, why do people always have to take the piss?"

I was confused. "Excuse me?"

"'Eve? You think I haven't heard that one hundred

times already? What next? You live in the garden of Eden?"

I glared at him. Those cobalt eyes now ice.

"My name is really Eve."

"Bullshit."

"Whatever. Just give me my bag. I want to go home."

He let the backpack dangle from his index finger for a second or two before he let it drop in front of his feet. We stared at each other. I realised he wouldn't budge and I all but stomped towards him. When I went to pick up my bag, he stopped me.

He seemed to study my face, his eyes so intense, I could tell he was trying to figure out if he could believe me. I reached into my coat pocket and flashed him my Oyster card: Eve Simpson.

His eyes darted from the card to my face and back again.

He cleared his throat.

"I'm sorry. Everyone takes the piss; I assumed someone put you up to it. I'm such a dick."

I was not about to disagree. In fact, I was ready to walk away when he stepped back and formally extended a hand.

"Hello Eve, I'm...Adam."

He was not kidding.

We laughed.

"Do you mind if I call you Evie?"

"I don't mind." I liked it.

The whole episode was funny.

It was fate.

. . .

WITH ADAM, it's always felt like he and I were meant to be. We clicked together like two missing parts, and discovered whole new sides to ourselves. Sometimes I joke that I was doomed to love Adam, but I guess that's what happens when you compound instant attraction and complete openness with one another. I never felt shy or ashamed to be me. Just me. Even the first time he saw me naked, even then—the two of us daring each other to swim in the icy lake one late autumn Saturday afternoon —I stripped down to my underwear without an ounce of fear that he would look away or laugh. No, the way he looked at me was quite the opposite. What I saw on his face was delight, and when I stepped out of my under-wear and tossed my tiny excuse for a bra onto the pebble beach, I delighted in seeing desire in his eyes. I remember how I teased him, and ran into the water, diving when it finally became deep enough, and screeching when the chill of the water shocked my body. I took a big gulp of air when I broke the water surface, and turned just in time to see him butt naked and running towards me, with border-line hysterics of yelling and laughing.

We swam towards each other and when we were close, I wrapped my legs and arms around him.

"You're so beautiful," he whispered, lips blue and chattering. I kissed him, tightening my limbs around him, making sure there wasn't an inch between us.

Not long after, we took the next step. Sex, just like every other aspect of our relationship, felt easy and natural. If we fumbled, we laughed about it, safe with each other. Safe to get it wrong, and safe to get it totally right.

But there was a problem with my birth control, and just three months after we became intimate, I missed a period. Scared of what would come next, of what my parents would do, I confided only in Adam.

"Let's be sure. It could be a false alarm. I'll buy a pregnancy test." Adam took control. And when that test came back positive, we decided together that an abortion was the only real option. We were too young to raise a baby, and there was no way in hell, Adam would ever give a child up for adoption.

We never told anyone. It was our secret. It knitted us close. But it also slowly festered, until it became the real reason for even the silliest of fights about not separating the recycling properly or not replacing the toilet roll.

I wander into the kitchen and check the recycling bins. Adam must have emptied them before he left, and for some reason this makes me start crying all over again.

TWO

ADAM

I'M PULLED into meetings most mornings, and the rest of the day is spent going over my kit and rewatching training videos on demonstrations on how the latest IEDs look. Improvised Explosive Devices are as nightmarish as they sound when you take just half a second to think about them. Basically, the Terrys will use anything they can lay their hands on to make bombs. And the horrific truth is that it doesn't take much. A bottle, a switch, and a small number of explosives readily available are literally all it takes. We use metal detectors to alert us to potential explosives, and then, because all of this happens in a giant sandpit, we use standard art paintbrushes to clear away the sand as gently as possible. If we can defuse at no to low risk, we do, but the alternative is much more fun. Sometimes we perform controlled explosions and detonate from a safe distance.

I'm busy repacking my man bag, which contains everything I need to do my job, when my mobile rings.

"Mr Taylor, this is Sandy Faro. You enquired about the cottage on our website? Are you still interested? Would you like to go and see it?"

"Hi. Yeah, I'm still interested, but I don't need to see it. I'd like to make an offer."

"You really should—it needs...quite a bit of work."

"I'm aware. I know the property. I live in the area."

I could hear that Sandy the estate agent was more than just a little surprised by my offer, not to mention relieved that I knew how much work the place needed. I didn't quibble on the price. I offered £10 000. She told me she would take it to the owner, but was sure it would be accepted.

"Hey, Pete!"

Pete looked up from his rifle; he had pulled it apart and was cleaning it methodically. "Yeah?"

"I bought the cottage, the one I showed you online."

"Yeah!" he just about roared as he jumped out of his seat and came over to pat me on the back. "Let's take our run past there this evening, yeah?"

"Sounds good. I just hope I didn't buy a fuckin' dud." But I'm smiling as I say it, because, when the deal is signed, I'll be a property owner. And maybe, just maybe I can be the guy who takes care of her the way she deserves.

LATER THAT DAY Pete stops dead in front of the cottage and then walks around the building. I'm still out of breath from the run, bent over with my hands on my knees, too scared to look up and face the reality of what I've bought.

"How bad is it?" I puff.

"Eh, not too bad, not too bad, but the roof—there's no saving that. I reckon you'll have to rip it off and ge' a new one. My cousin has a roof business; he'll give you a good price."

When I do look up, I see the collapsing roof and my heart sinks. He's right.

"It's not so bad," he reassures me with a slap on the back. "You know what you need?"

"A refund?"

"No, an architect, to help you visualise the space."

"I don't need an architect. I know exactly how I want the layout to look."

I don't tell him Evie and I used to lay out imaginary rooms here when we were kids. An open-plan kitchen with a large hearth on the west wall for the lounge. Dining room to the right and her art studio at the back, because it has the best afternoon light. Three bedrooms upstairs. A lavish antique bathtub concluded our fantasy.

Pete throws his hands up. "Well, in that case, let me buy you a pint."

This time I don't pass up the opportunity to commiserate...or celebrate. Only time will tell which one it will be.

One pint turns into two with a couple of Jack Daniels

shots to round off the night. Not surprisingly, my internal homing device defaults to going home.

I beat the fire-engine red door with a fist until she opens it. I can tell she hasn't been asleep. Her hair is up in a messy bun and there's blue and white paint on her hands. She has been working on her new landscape series, no doubt. She's wearing my old Def Leppard T-shirt and seemingly nothing else. It's stock from the late nineties, a stretched-out, faded relic that never made the charity pile for sentimental reasons. I'm a little tipsy from drinking with Pete, enough to find it amusing that she ended up keeping one of my favourite T-shirts while I ended up with a check shirt I hate, but not so pissed that I'm blind to just how damn sexy she is wearing it.

As if she can read my mind, she tugs the shirt down, but even then it hardly covers the red lace panties peeking out.

"What are you doing here? You're pissed!" She's shout-whispering, eyes darting left and right at the neighbouring houses.

I step closer, dragging my gaze from her shapely legs to the lush fullness of her bottom lip. Evie has always turned heads with her fiery hair, but for me, it's her mouth, always indicative of her mood and so indescribably sensual that it drives me crazy.

"Adam, you shouldn't be here." She takes a step back as I take another forward. My trainers are no more than an inch from the threshold. I'm so close, I can smell the faint bouquet of her perfume which still lingers in her hair mixed with paint and turpentine. She smells like home. No, she *is* home and all I want to do is lose myself in her. I pull her face to mine and stifle her gasp when I take over her mouth with my own. Then I'm over the threshold, pressing her against the wall as our tongues dart and collide. My lips find their way to the soft spot of her earlobe, and she lets out a low moan that makes me forget about everything else, except kissing her. I ravish her neck like a starving person at a buffet and I feel her body give. For a few more feverish seconds, we're just us, without the BS.

"Adam. A-dam!"

She's pushing me away. We stop, both breathless. My eyes search hers. I know we shouldn't be doing this, but I'm deploying in the morning and I need her. I. Need. Her. I always have.

Her lips part and she draws a breath to speak. I wait. I hope she can see everything I want to say in my eyes, because words, I have none. She makes her decision. Her lips crash on mine, and all at once, she's in my arms and I'm carrying her to our bed.

Evie

GOD KNOWS I've never been able to resist Adam. Not when I was an awkward teenager making sense of my new woman's body. And not now. When he kisses me, I'm fifteen, sixteen, seventeen all over again.

It took Adam a long time to kiss me back then. So long, that I got impatient and decided to make it happen. Well, I tried. I scooted up to him at the back of an almost empty bus on the way home from school one rainy afternoon. Eyes closed, lips puckered, slick with watermelon-flavoured gloss, I went in full throttle with the recklessness reserved for teenagers. Instead of finding the long-sought-after sensation of his lips, something I'd been daydreaming about for more than a month already, and practicing on the bathroom mirror and the back of my hand, I was met with his open palm.

My eyes flew open. Instant regret flushed my cheeks to match my fiery hair. He looked at me quizzically, as if he wanted to make sense of my actions, and then when he connected the dots of my lips zooming in on his, his expression defragmented to a face neutral and incapable of showing emotion. And then he turned away.

I inched away from him, bit by bit, until there was a whole seat between us. I stared out of the misted-up window even though I couldn't really see out. We never spoke nor looked at each other until we both got off at Gander Green Lane.

"I'm sorry," I said, finally finding the courage to look into his cornflower-blue eyes.

He shook his head. "No, I'm sorry. I'm an idiot."

"I shouldn't have—"

"You caught me by surprise, that's all." He was studying me so intently, my knees felt like jelly. I gulped. Now what? Neither of us moved. He raised an eyebrow as if to say 'come on then', and I appreciated his dimpled grin, daring me to be the one to make the first move. But now it was me who wasn't ready. The moment was too immense. I cleared my throat.

"Do you want to come for tea?" I asked gingerly.

He nodded, conceding that the moment had passed. Or so I thought. We walked alongside each other, his hand grazing mine every so often, until we reached the split in the road. It was then that he grabbed my hand, forcing me to turn and face him.

"I'm ready now," he said, stepping closer, so close I could smell the spicy smell of AXE. His lips hovered over mine,

"Me too," I said. And then he kissed me.

NOW HERE WE ARE, him in my arms, his lips on my neck, even though I chucked him out of my house and my life just days ago. For a nanosecond I hesitate, knowing full well that us having sex would only complicate our break-up. But fucking hell, the man is my magnet.

He carries me down the passage to our room without any effort, and it's one of the things I love about him. How I've always felt protected and safe with him. He lays me down on the bed tenderly, despite how full-on our kissing is. Within seconds I've shed the T-shirt and his weight is on me, knee parting my thighs. It's our tango and we know all the moves. I'm breathless as his lips work their way down my throat, pause at the dip between my collar bones, and then his tongue takes over and snakes a gratifying trail to my navel. He teases the hollow with his tongue, and my back arches with the spike of pleasure coursing through my veins like lava.

"You like that," he whispers, and he tortures me some more while small, muffled groans escape his busy mouth.

"God, you're so hot when you're turned on," he says as his face resurfaces and comes to meet mine.

"I want you." His voice is thick with desire, and I know what he's actually asking is am I sure I want this, too. He's always been this way. I'm the China doll he's afraid he'll break.

"I want *you*," I assure him. We seal our agreement with a deep kiss that soon becomes desperate.

He kisses my chin and moves on to find my nipples hard and eager. He greets them with tongue and teeth in turn, causing me to whimper. The ache to be filled by him, to have him inside me, is carnal.

"I want you inside me," I beg.

Now it's his turn to chuckle and I know it means *not yet.*

We make eye contact a moment before the warm pressure of his mouth covers my swollen and throbbing clit. I catch my breath as my hips buck in response to the heat. I pull his head closer and push myself more to meet him, inhibitions dissolving at a rapid rate. Waves of pleasure wash over me as he laps at me through the flimsy lace constraint.

Jesusfuckingchrist, I'm going to explode.

And then the lace is pushed aside and he's on me, in me—lips, tongue.

I'm unravelling, at the precipice of the delicious free fall, into a void of pleasure.

"Oh, God, ohgod ohgod ohgod."

And just as he pushes me to the edge of my orgasm, he pulls me back. He lifts his head and I groan, lifting my head to beg him not to stop. Before I can say anything, he's covering my body with his own, and his mouth comes crashing down on mine. I can taste my musk and feel his erection pressed against my pussy all at once, and just like that, my body writhes beneath him of its own volition. His breathing is low and erratic now, and I know I won't have to wait much longer.

I lift his face to meet me eye to eye. "Please," I beg. His cornflower eyes are bright with desire.

"Evie..." It's barely audible, so thick with want is his voice.

The lace barrier is discarded first, and then he stands at the foot of the bed and strips off his clothes. I devour the sight of him, my arousal pushed up another notch at the sight of the definition of abs and pecs. I won't lie, the army made that body strong and sculpted. But it's the bulge of his biceps and the visible triceps on his sculpted arms that make it impossible for me to look away. My name, Evie, tattooed on his left shoulder. He is mine and I am his.

His jeans and boxers fall to the floor in a single heap, and a second later the length of his body is hovering over mine. Our bodies shift to accommodate our coming together, his cock nuzzling its place at my slick entrance. I slide under him, eager to have him inside me at last.

"I love you," he whispers, dropping the softest of kisses on my forehead. He doesn't wait for me to reply as he thrusts his cock inside me so hard, I cry out in glorious agony of being stretched and filled. He groans, too, a base, animalistic sound that makes my hips rise to accommodate all of him.

There's no slowing down. There's no more thinking.

His fingers are gripping the flesh on my hips. He pulls out and rams into me—hard—again and again, and I never want him to stop. He lifts my legs over his right shoulder, as he ploughs inside me. I'm so close; he is so so deep.

"Adam, oh God."

I feel his release inside me, and he buries his cock in even deeper, hugging my knees to his chest. It pushes me over the edge, and a frantic jolt of climatic spasms means that we are riding this wave together. We're breathing hard as we come down, and I'm eager for his kiss when he comes to settle beside me. I wrap my arms around his neck, my legs snaked with his.

We don't speak. There's too much to say.

THREE

ADAM

I WAKE with Evie curled against my back, her arm loose with sleep over me. It's early, my army clock already set for deployment. I know I need to leave now or I'll be shovelling shit for missing inspections before they load us like cattle into buses and then military aircraft destined for Fort Bastion in Afghanistan.

I slide out of bed without waking her, and I can't help but smile, seeing her face so content. She always sleeps like the dead. Way back, when we were attending a family wedding in Australia, there was an earthquake in the night, a 6.6 on the Richter. I bolted out of bed just in time to catch the room's coffee percolator from falling off the shelf, while Evie's response was to roll over and carry on snoring.

I find most of my clothes on the floor and dress

quickly. I give my sleeping Evie a gentle kiss on the fore-head before letting myself out.

From the house to the base is a ten-minute walk, and I pick up my walking pace in the smudgy darkness, the first etching of daylight still just a glow on the horizon. If I was a more romantic man, I would have left Evie a note, which is only marginally better from what I've just done —left without saying good morning or goodbye.

I pull my phone out of my pocket, relieved to find I still have ten percent battery to record a voice note. It's not ideal, I know. I really should have woken her. She's going to be less than impressed with me when she surfaces, that's for sure, so I better make this good. I take a deep breath and try not to overthink it and just start talking.

"Hey, Evie... Do you remember the day we met? I know we relay the story, about how I thought you were taking the piss when you told me your name, to anyone who cares about our story...but for me, the thing I remember clearly is the moment I saw you. It was *not* while I was in line, during cadets, in the quad that day. I noticed you in the cafeteria at lunch. You walked in and stopped in the entrance, looked around—the line was long and impossible that day—and you walked out. You were holding a stack of books in front of you like a shield. I noticed your freckles first and then when you spun round to walk away, I saw your legs and I thought, those calves must play tennis...

"Turned out, they, the calves I mean, played netball, but that did not stop you from beating me at many games of squash later—but only because your legs are so distracting, definitely *not* because you are the better player...

"When it comes to you I've always been a shallow bastard. I was drawn to you instantly, and when I saw you, I wanted to walk over and say hello. Badly. And so, when you stood staring at me in the quad, I really did feel your eyes on me. I don't know how to explain it, except to say that I felt like someone had jolted me with an electric rod and I was suddenly alive. You saw me. I'd never felt that way before. This is a recurring theme for me when it comes to us. You always *see* me. Inside me. Up until that point in my life, I'd felt invisible, or, worked hard at being under the radar... Moving around between foster homes will do that to you. You learn the hard way to lay low, almost unnoticed, so that you're not a nuisance to the well-meaning folk who have taken you in, not just out of charity, but also for the free money they get from Her Majesty.

"You seeing me is the single best thing that has ever happened to me.

"I'm sorry I left without waking you to say goodbye... You were so peaceful...and the truth is I was too afraid you'd wake up and...

I love you, Evie. Don't forget it."

When I reach the base, I break into a run. I don't have much time to get showered and kitted up for the final inspections before it's Go Time.

THE LAST LEG of the flight to Fort Bastion, in the Helmand Province of Afghanistan, is brutal. Sixty minutes of squatting in a Chinook made for twenty, but now with the seats ripped out, forty of us are crammed in any which way we fit—kits and all. I scratch Fosters behind the ears, and pat her to calm her down; the weapons and ammunition strapped to our bodies aren't helping her settle, not to mention the sticky air that's getting staler by the second.

I stand up when the loadmaster calls ten minutes to landing. I make eye contact with the seven other members of my squad, each in turn, and call-sign KILLJOY 22. We give each other a nod, indicating we're ready. Pete is closer to the door than I am, and I watch him click his neck from side to side, his tell that he's raring to go.

Five minutes until we touch down. The energy is electric and there's so much adrenaline and testosterone in the aircraft, you can smell it. The moment we hit the ground, the mad rush to get out starts, and I stumble before I'm back on my feet and running into the darkness which swallows us up one by one. While the black night serves as some sort of cover, an aircraft on the ground is an easy target for the Taliban, and it's crucial that we disperse as fast as possible so that the aircraft can take off safely. When I've cleared some distance, I pull my night-vision goggles, NVGs for short, from my daysack which hangs in front of my body for easy access. In here I have the essentials: wire cutters, smoke grenades, my personal protection pistol, morphine, and a paintbrush.

Mentally, I'm constantly going over and cross-checking

my gear in my head. The paintbrush is always packed at the very top for easy access. I'm no artist like Evie; it's just that over the years we've found that gentle brush strokes with an ordinary artist's brush are the best tool to sweep away the sand that covers absolutely everything in this part of the world. The latest home-cooked explosives the Terry's have hidden in the hopes of blowing the troops to smithereens should not be underestimated, and I want eyes on every angle and wire before I decide how to disarm it.

Still keeping our heads down, we run east. We have about a kilometre to cover before we reach cover and our base for the next six months. I turn to see my boys following me, all of them visible by the little red dot on the side of their NVGs. I raise my hand and signal a halt, and they gather in a semicircle, one knee to the ground.

"Everyone okay? We have nine hundred metres, give or take, before we reach camp. Take a breather now, because when we get going, we're not stopping till we get there. We will not be sitting ducks for the Terry's. Got it?"

"Sir!" Collective agreement.

"Hydrate. We're moving in five."

I take a drink of water myself and a deep breath of the cool night air, grateful that there's some relief from the heat my body is generating with the extra forty-five kgs of kit I'm carrying. I assess my crew and see Thomas wiping the sweat from his forehead repeatedly, like a twitch.

"Dickens"—Pete comes up beside me—"Thomas, he isn't looking good."

I nod. "Yeah, let's bring him upfront with me. You take the back with Jackson."

"Let's go, boys! Thomas, you're with me."

It's too risky to march it, so I start the run and set the pace with Thomas's footfall behind mine. About halfway I'm feeling it. The kit is heavy and our uniform is thick and weighty, as well. I'd curse if I had enough air, but everything I've got is going into keeping us moving. I hear Pete's whistle; he'll whistle for my attention instead of calling out in situations like this one. I turn my head to look over my shoulder and see that with all my huffing and puffing, I missed the fact that Thomas was falling behind. I stop and wait for him to catch up. His thin, matchstick legs are literally buckling under the weight, and in an effort to speed up, his knees give way and he folds as he reaches me.

I raise my hand to stop the rest who are jogging in single file behind us.

"Devereaux," I call Thomas by his surname as I kneel beside him, "talk to me."

The kid is struggling for breath. He's only nineteen, this is his first mission, and I can tell that shit has gotten properly real for him. I remember that feeling, but there's no time for pep talks and singing 'Kumbaya'; we absolutely have to keep moving.

"I can't, I can't." He's out of breath.

"You have one minute to get yourself together. Give me your backpack."

He looks at me, eyes bewildered. "No! No, I can't do that!"

I reach over to unclip the strap across his chest. "You can and you will."

"Sir..." He wants to protest but there's no point, and I'm certain he already knows how hard the others are going to rag him when we get to base. When I pull the bag off his back, I wince. It's easily fifty kilos, but the relief on Thomas's strained face is immediate.

"Fucking hell, Devereaux, whatever's in here better be worth it."

We start moving again, slower this time, because I'm weighed down by the extra pack, but after what seems like the longest five hundred metres in world history, we make it to the gates of Bastion and the welcoming smell of hot grub.

Evie

IT'S BEEN two weeks since Adam deployed and I still haven't listened to the voice note he left. I'm angry that, despite my pleas for him to stay, despite our night together, he left anyway.

I haven't listened to it and I haven't deleted it.

If I'm totally honest with myself, I'm also afraid that if I do listen to it, my resolve to end our relationship will crumble and I'll just end up waiting for him again. I love him, that hasn't changed, but I'll be damned if I wait around another six months, another year. My father wasn't right about a lot of the things he said to me at Christmas, but the fact that I'm always the one waiting, living alone for half the year, sometimes longer, wasn't a word of a lie.

His leaving never gets easier, only harder. Nothing prepares me for the heartbreaking goodbyes—the uncertainty and fear, that this may very well be the final cup of tea together, the final kiss. I was stupid when I was younger. Adam's first tour was imbued with romance. Long love letters would arrive no more than two weeks after he left. And he'd call every opportunity available. I told my friends my boyfriend was fighting for his country overseas. I turned down dates to formals and hanging out with the girls, just to be home and watch the phone, willing it to ring. I missed so much of my own life while Adam was out living his. But then he would come back and I would run into my soldier's arms and find that no matter how long we were forced to be apart, he was my home. I told him that once when he had just returned from one of his first tours. Already the toll it had taken on him was visible in more pronounced lines around his mouth that made him look stern all the time.

"You're my home," I whispered while wrapped in his arms after we'd made love.

He was quiet.

"Evie, there's something...you're my home, too. And that's why..." His voice trailed off and he cleared his throat. For a split second, I thought: this is it, he's going to ask me to marry him!

"Yes?" I said, turning onto my side so that I looked at him properly, and he did the same. I took the moment in; I wanted to remember every detail of our engagement story to tell our children one day. His eyes were that impossible blue of a clear spring sky. I touched the day-old stubble on his face that made him look ruggedly handsome. He closed his eyes for a second before he asked me.

"Will you be my next of kin?"

THE MEMORY IS SO painful that I find myself wincing and having to ask my mum to repeat the question.

"Has he called?" Mum asks again, and I picture her sitting in her conservatory with a cup of tea while we speak on the phone.

"No, Mum. You know he can't. No mobiles on the job." Except if there's bad news. I don't remind her of that, though.

"So, it's over?"

I sigh. "I guess so. Yes."

"Do you want to come and stay with us for a while? Dad will be so happy to have you. I could clear the loft, and you could work up there—there's lots of light."

"Sure," I agree without overthinking it. I could use a change of scenery. My new exhibit is coming up in two months at the Tate Britain. My mentor from university sits on the board of the gallery and has invited me to fill the spot of another artist who has had to withdraw last-minute. It's a massive opportunity, but I'm feeling the pressure to deliver, and maybe being at Mum's will help ease that.

"Wonderful!" Mum sounds so pleased it's almost

heartbreaking. I haven't seen them since Christmas, some three months ago.

"Oh, darling, it'll be so much fun. And then we can talk about Adam. I'm sure you two can work it out."

"No, Mum." I stop her in her tracks. She's always fawned over Adam, unlike Dad who has only ever tolerated him with ladles of suspicion. I know Mum's heart's broken; thirteen years is a long time to get attached to a faux son, but I'm not going to allow her to influence my decision.

"Adam and I are done. Clearly, we want different things; it's time to let go." As much as I'm trying to be assertive, my voice wobbles at the end.

"Evie?"

"Mum, please, I want to come and see you, but I won't stay if you keep harping on about Adam, okay?"

Mum pauses, and I can imagine her looking up at the ceiling, taking a moment to weigh up how serious she thinks I'm being before she agrees, "Okay."

After we hang up, I go back to my chat history with Adam and see the message waiting for me. My finger hovers over the PLAY arrow, but instead, I toss the phone aside, turn up the volume on some 90s classics, pick up a brush, and head to an empty canvas.

FOUR

ADAM

THE COMPOUND IS an arrangement of large, white tents, like you'd find at outdoor weddings, closed off by a five-foot-thick and twelve-foot-high cement wall. Some of the office areas are air-conditioned so that the computers don't fry, and even though there are cafes and a gym, it's a far cry from home. This is where we wait for the call for our next mission. In the six weeks we've been here, we've already disposed of twenty-three IEDs—that's nearly four per day.

I walk into the Ops room to get our orders and Major Cline is standing behind his desk shuffling papers. Behind him, I see a map of Afghan, red dots marking all the places where we've found bombs, and worse, as well as spots where there have been explosions.

"Major." I salute.

"Dickens, have a seat."

I do as I'm told, perching at the edge, hands clasped with forearms resting on my knees. My gut tells me this is going to be a biggie.

The major finds what he's looking for, pushes his glasses back up onto the bridge of his nose, and sits down.

"We've had intel that there's work to be done at the Dutch outpost. Your team leaves in an hour."

"That's it?"

Major eyes me over his spectacles.

"You'll be briefed in full on arrival, Staff Sergeant. Is there a problem?"

"No, sir."

"Dismissed."

I'm less than impressed with the lack of details provided, and it must show on my face because when I walk into the rec room and find Pete, he immediately asks me what's the matter.

"We leave in fifty minutes—get the guys together."

"Where to?"

"Fuck knows. I guess we'll find out when we get there. All I know is that we're going to the Dutch post."

Overhearing us, private Daniel Stewart gives a whoop of excitement. Daniel was christened 'Little' after *Stuart Little,* the movie. The guys can be brutal with their nicknames, and when Daniel showed up as lanky as a bean pole, with a head of ash-white hair and matching whiskers, sparsely spread, it just took one bloke to make the connection. Little took it in his stride, I'll give him that.

"What are you getting excited about, Little?"

"I'm looking forward to the great grub!"

"Just get your arse in gear and let's get moving," Pete reprimands him. We watch Little scurry off but can't help but smile at each other when he's out of sight.

"If there's one fing we love about the Dutch," Pete says, "it's their little balls."

I chuckle. "They are called croquettes," I correct him. "I hear their squad leader is a woman. Not many of those around in the army out in the field."

"She must have a pair to keep the men in check."

"I bet."

TIME IN AFGHAN IS RELATIVE. Sometimes it's stretched and slow like liquid mercury sliding off the edge of the table. The waiting can drag. We end up playing ping-pong for hours, talking shit and smoking too much. I've never admitted to smoking to Evie—she'd hate it—but I think she knows. She's not stupid. All that gum I chew for the first couple of weeks after a tour must be a dead giveaway.

And just as much as time can really slow down, in Afghan everything seems to happen all at once. One minute you're lying in your army cot in your pants under a fan, trying not to die of heatstroke, and the next you're pulling on your boots and climbing in a helicopter, flying over Helmand. The adrenalin roller coaster is real, and army guys live for the thrills. That's the thing about the army, it's a calling for a certain type.

A. Violent childhood.

B. Abused.

C. Raised without knowing fatherly affection.

D. Poor.

E. No interest in school subjects.

F. Reckless. Adrenaline junkie.

Most of us are at least a 4/6, but if we're 100 percent honest with ourselves, we're all 6/6. We all have a story we'd rather forget. So we gravitate towards the hard shit: excessive physical training, pushing our bodies to the limit in dangerous situations. Having grown up poor, adapting to wearing one set of clothes for most of your life and getting by with a tiny paycheck is simply what we're used to.

But for all the piss-taking and malarkey back at the base, while we were in limbo, the squad is silent and focused in the chopper. We fly north, and the view of the province from the air is breathtaking. The Helmand River snakes down the middle of the desert; lush green embankments on either side mean farms: wheat and opium poppy. Although we can't hear them, the kids playing on the river banks jump and wave at the helicopter. I'm always slightly taken aback when I see parts of Afghanistan from the air—it's beautiful. And it's hard to imagine how riddled with violence it really is.

The Dutch outpost is in south Afghan in the Uruzgan Province. It takes the chopper a little over an hour to fly the two-hundred and sixty kilometres and deliver us to the Dutch. In that time I'm mentally preparing for what lies ahead, playing out various scenarios in my head. Once again I open my cross-body bag and make sure all my equipment is organised for fast and easy access. Wire cutters, tape, smoke grenades, paintbrush...Evie.

Before I can stop myself, I've conjured an image of her in my mind's eye. She's up in the loft where we've put in windows and skylights so that no matter the time of day, the light is just right. She's sitting on a high stool, working on the finest detail with a delicate brush. She is beautiful in her personal habitat. Messy hair tied up in an absentminded bun. Is that what she's doing now? For a split second my fantasy is fractured by the flash of an image of her with another man. Fuck. The fact that she hadn't picked up my voice note before I had to switch off my mobile and hand it in, is eating me alive. Are we really over? Was our last night together final breakup sex?

Pete elbows me, which brings me back to the present at the same time that we get the 'ten minutes till landing' call. I go through the contents of my bag again. I'm as ready as I'll ever be; no doubt we'll hit the ground running.

There's a truck waiting for us when we land, and a soldier with another close behind strides towards us.

"Staff!" he greets me by my rank.

"Van der Land." I extend a hand, reading his name on his left breast pocket.

"Welcome to Kamp Holland."

I nod, and immediately a female officer joins and introduces herself.

"Lieutenant Katja Janssen."

"Staff Sergeant Adam Taylor." I salute her. "How can we help?"

She gets straight to business. "One of our supply

trucks was ambushed this morning. We think the Terry's have worked out the routes we take. We drive a different route each time, but either they got lucky or they've been watching us very closely. We have two critically injured who have been airlifted for medical treatment."

"Take us to the location, and we'll do a sweep, and clean up what we can."

The back of the truck is not the most comfortable and the open back kicks up a hell of a lot of dust, so for most of the thirty-minute ride, we sit with our heads down, sweating like pigs being bumped and jiggled around as we cover rough terrain.

When we reach the location of the incident, it's already cordoned off with makeshift barriers. The sight of the bombed truck, burnt black and in fragments, strewn like confetti for metres all around, is upsetting if you spend more than ten seconds thinking about the harsh reality of it all. A couple of our crew bring their cotton scarves to their faces, covering their noses and mouths from the smell. While Lieutenant Janssen hadn't divulged the extent of the injuries of her men, it's obvious at least one of them was badly burned.

"Okay, boys, this is how we're going to do it," I say and I run through our next steps. Pete and I will walk up front, two metres apart, side by side, scanning the area. The rest will be split and follow single file, either behind Pete or I, doing the same. The slightest beep and we stop and assess.

Slowly we make our way towards the upside-down truck, heat still radiating from the burnt metal. Twenty meters past the spot of the ambush, we stop. Pete's rod has found something.

"Not very clear—could be nuffing," Pete calls to me.

"Wait for me."

I keep my strides short, with the wheel of the metal detector only about a ruler's length ahead of my steps.

When I reach Pete, I kneel down and slowly and very gently start digging around the hotspot until the container holding the explosives comes into view. It's an empty, plastic milk carton. Pete lets out a low whistle.

"A blinkin' milk carton! No wonder the me'al detector didn't go crazy. They've hidden it in plastic."

"Yeah." I reach for my brush and start dusting the sand on the top. Now the IED is in full view and I can see the wires exposed where the cap of the bottle should be.

"Step back, mate, and tell the lads to keep their distance. I'm going to clip this one."

I hear Pete call the command to the men to stand clear. The sweat is dripping from my brow, and as I gently separate the wires, all I can hear is my blood beating hard in my ears. A few times I have to stop and remember to breathe, but as soon as I have the wires untangled, I look over my shoulder to check that our men are far enough away, just in case I clip the wrong wire.

Which I won't, I remind myself.

I hesitate just a moment when I have the wire in the mouth of the clippers, and then I squeeze it decisively.

Snip.

I relax from the tense kneeling position and plonk myself down on my backside while I take a moment to remove my eye protection and wipe the sweat from my face. The guys let out a cheer, and there are a couple of whistles and claps directed at me.

I raise a hand.

"Little! Devereaux! Get your sorry arses here and come do some work for a change!"

Minutes later, when the IED has been exhumed, I use red spray paint and spray a circle around the hole in the ground, marking the place from which we unearthed the bomb.

"Bag it," I remind Little. "We need to show HQ this one."

We spend another four hours scanning the area with metal detectors, following the route the drivers would take going to and from the Dutch base camp. We find three more bombs planted about five hundred metres apart. The Taliban have booby-trapped the road. Only when we clear a full kilometre from the last IED, do we call it a day.

***

"I SUGGEST your supply truck find at least three more different routes to travel from now on," I tell Janssen later that evening over a plate of food. "Now that they know of the one we cleared today, they'll keep coming back."

Lieutenant Katja Janssen nods. Without her military cap on, and her long, blonde hair pulled back in a pony-tail, she seems young. Her blue eyes captivate when she talks to you; she is intense. I realise that, as a woman, even in the twenty-first century, she must have worked her tail off to get where she is, but it's not hard to see how she manages to command. I look over, and Pete, who could be a meme for 'hanging on every word', has his mouth slightly open and eyes large and glued to our female colleague. I can't help but smile.

"Pete," I say, "perhaps you can help the Lieutenant plot out a couple of new routes? He's a map geek," I direct at Janssen.

"Could you? That would be absolutely awesome."

"No problem, Serg."

"Call me Katja." I watch a smile pass between them before Pete is on his feet, rattling on about using dry river beds as seasonal roads and Katja leading the way to the Ops room.

Well now. My man Pete has a prospect.

Evie

MUM COMES upstairs to the loft where I'm working.

I arrived on Thursday, thinking a long weekend with the folks would be just what the doctor ordered. For the first day I was here, I didn't bother bringing my art supplies out of the boot of my car, not until I was sure Dad was going to behave himself. I can't deal with the 'good riddance' speech about Adam. I've ignored his self-satisfied demeanour, at having gotten his way regarding Adam, for Mum's sake, and so far, he has been sweet as honey. He even gave me his credit card when Mum and I hit the High Street on Friday morning, and Mum helped me choose a pretty, emerald-green blouse that's too fancy for my day job, but it complements my complexion and will dress up nicely for my exhibition.

"Darling, don't forget the Whites are coming to dinner tonight. You must remember them—he's a podiatrist."

"Mmm."

Mum puts a hand on my shoulder. "Well, isn't that coming along nicely?"

I turn to see Mum openly admiring my work.

"What's it called?"

"This one is called Herefordshire Winter."

"Evie, your landscapes capture the light and mood perfectly. Is that the abandoned cottage near the river?"

"It is."

I don't tell her it's Adam's and my cottage, the place we laid claim to when we were kids. How many summer evenings did we meet there to be alone? Too many to count. I have vivid memories of lying on a blanket, looking up at the stars with Adam.

"What are you thinking about?" he asked me while running his fingers up and down my bare arm. Goose-flesh rippled throughout my body, sending sensations between my legs that made me dizzy.

I giggled, because I was a girl becoming familiar with lust, and because I wasn't thinking of anything else except him and how good the weight of his body would feel on top of mine.

He chuckled, and I remember wondering if he was feeling it too.

"What are you thinking of?" I retorted, daring him to name what was happening between us.

He propped himself up onto his elbow and dipped his head to kiss me, but his lips stayed suspended just millimetres away from mine. It was a cruel, delicious game, and I was ready to eat.

"I'm thinking," he murmured, so close I got heady with the sweet smell of his breath, "I'm thinking of how it would feel to touch you."

Fingers brushed over the hard buttons of my nipples in my tank top, and floated farther south to the swollen bud between my thighs. So light was his touch, that it must have been impossible to feel it with the denim layer covering me, but I found myself gasping. He silenced me with a deep kiss, his hand gained confidence, and I responded by arching my hips and rubbing myself against it. I moaned and his lips trailed my neck to a place just below my earlobe, which made me moan louder. And then I orgasmed, seeing the stars that I'd only read about in my mum's Mills and Boon collection.

IN THE PRESENT MOMENT, I swallow hard, trying my best to suppress the memories of us at that cottage, the place where Adam unlocked a part of me that has been his ever since.

We both take a moment. Mum's eyes stay focused on the canvas, and I notice that the fine lines around her eyes are a bit deeper. Living with Dad isn't easy, and I know she's been worried about me and Adam too.

"Are you alright?"

"I'm fine, sweetheart." She gives me a smile I know well—one that doesn't quite reach the eyes. Sad but full of resolve.

"Mum, you can talk to me. Is it Dad?"

She shrugs. "Nothing new there. He's a stubborn old fart, stuck in his ways. I've been worried about you."

"But I'm fine. You can see that, can't you?"

She gives me that marble smile again, beautiful but cold. "Of course."

"I really am okay. And if it's Adam you're worried about, I'm sure he is okay too. He's a grown man. He'll figure his life out."

She nods, but I can see she doesn't believe me. Her affection for Adam goes beyond her just liking him. She's told me more than once how lucky I was to meet a man who adores me so openly. Hers and Dad's relationship has always been stale but impenetrable, and while Mum plays the part of the doting wife, Dad relishes his role as the emotionally distant man of the house. Where public displays of affection have been lacking, Dad has always been inclined to grand gestures, such as, a new car, or week-long Italian cooking classes and wine tasting in Tuscany, on special occasions. Even with all the stuff and experiences, and twenty-seven years of marriage, Mum still craves his tangible affection.

Adam's warmth towards me has always been physical. We could never be near each other without touching. It annoyed my father when Adam would get up from the dinner table for a glass of water and drop a peck on my cheek as he did so.

"You're just going to the kitchen, for God's sake, not Timbuktu."

And Adam's response? "You never know what could happen between the dining room and kitchen. I could keel over, and at least, I would have kissed the love of my life as my last meaningful act on Earth."

Is that why he came knocking the night before he deployed? He wanted the last meaningful time we had together to be amazing in case the worst happened?

"Is there any chance you'll take Adam back?"

"No. I don't think so. I think Dad is right; I can't sit around waiting all the time. It's been thirteen years and he hasn't asked me to marry him. I'm not sure he ever will."

Mum nods and her tone adjusts. "Dad has said you should wear that new blouse tonight, and don't be late. Drinks on the patio at six sharp. He wants to make a good impression on the Whites."

"You make it sound like a networking event, or worse, a job interview."

"You know how your father is."

No doubt about that.

———

AT 5:45 my mobile rings and I answer without checking who it is, hitting the speaker button.

"It's quarter to six—tell me you are showered and getting ready for drinks."

"Mum? Did you just call me from the kitchen?" I

hear pots clanging and Dad interjecting in the background.

"Yes. I can't leave the onion tart. These last few minutes are crucial. Just tell me you're ready to come downstairs—your father is getting antsy."

I look around the loft, the chaos that is my art, and then I look at my paint-stained hands.

"I'll be there—give me a minute," I say and I hang up before she starts panicking even more.

I sigh. The light is perfect now; it's a pity to have to down tools. I wipe the bushes with a damp, turpentine cloth, and leave them in water to clean before I run to my childhood bedroom to do a quick strip-wash, change into an old but pretty enough summer's dress, and manage a lick of mascara and lipstick before I meet my parents in the garden at six on the dot.

"There she is!" My father is jolly, and when he kisses me on the cheek, I smell the whiskey on his breath. Mum got into the habit of mellowing him out before parties with a stiff drink before guests arrive.

"Prosecco?"

"Beer, if you have." I smile sweetly and end up taking the flute of bubbles he puts in my hand.

"Don't be ridiculous," my father puffs.

Not a minute later and the doorbell echoes through the house. I stay put while Dad, in his cream, linen trousers and plain, white, short-sleeve, collared shirt, scurries off to greet the guests.

"Joan, Charles, you remember my daughter Evelyn?"

I hear him introduce me by my christened name. The

only person who called me that was my French teacher. I get up to correct him.

"Please, call me Evie, everyone does," I say, and when I'm standing in front of them with my hand extended, I see that Mr and Mrs White MD are not alone. They've brought, I can only assume, their single son along.

"This is Gerald. I think you last saw him in the sand-pit! It's no wonder he's such an up-and-coming architect —it was obvious even back then—always building the biggest sandcastles." Dad laughs, a little too loudly.

In an instant, I feel the heat in my cheeks as anger flushes through me. What was this, a bloody playdate?

Then I look at Mum, who can't look me in the eye. She suddenly dashes off to do something urgent in the kitchen.

Gerald steps forward from behind his parents, looking even more mortified than I am, but he manages a smile that's all veneers and money when he puts out his hand.

I take it, but my smile is so tight, my teeth so clenched, I don't manage a word.

"My parents tell me you're an artist?"

I look over and see the conspirators, Dad and Mrs White, smiling and raising a glass in our direction as they make themselves comfortable at the table, while I'm left to make small talk with my blind date.

I down the contents of my glass in one, long sip.

"What the fuck is going on?" I hiss.

"Apparently it's time I got married. You're a catch I'm told," he says. And I see him scan my outfit and un-pedi-cured, sandalled feet with open disapproval.

I snicker but am strangely comforted by the fact that Gerald isn't really seeing me as his potential future bride.

"More fizz?" he points to my empty glass.

"Come with me."

He obeys without asking questions and follows me into the house. Just once I look over my shoulder and swear I see my father give me a wink of encouragement. I could explode.

Gerald dutifully follows me to the drinks cabinet and I pull out a bottle of tequila hidden behind the rows of Scotch. I pull the cork and without thinking twice, I take a huge gulp. The shock of fire in my mouth hits hard, and I scrunch up my face and try to catch my breath as I hand over the bottle to Gerald. Gerald looks over his shoulder to make sure we're not being watched and then, like me, throws the alcohol back with abandon. He coughs and splutters, and jumps around a bit while he swallows. I laugh. I take the bottle from him and carefully replace it. I smooth down my hair, and then my dress, and then this new stranger, who was thrust into my life, and I have a good look at each other.

He is handsome. Polished. On the short side, but slender. A long, blond fringe is fashionably flicked to the side. His eyes are ice blue, pale but attractive. His outfit is perfect for the summer evening: white shorts and a baby-pink golf shirt. And I notice his hands are soft and nails manicured.

I immediately become self-conscious about my own, rough painter's hands and short fingernails, probably with paint under them. Instinctively I check. Yup. Green acrylic. I cringe.

Gerald speaks first. "I can see why my mother thinks you and I could...get along. You're pretty enough. Creative. A few nice pieces of clothes, a new haircut, and a mani-pedi, and you'll be just right."

I narrow my eyes and feel my blood starting to boil all over again.

"Don't worry, honey, you're not my type." He gives me a cheeky wink.

Of course, there's a very good reason Gerald hasn't found himself in the realm of holy matrimony.

"You haven't come out?"

"Mummy knows, but Daddy wouldn't understand— too old-school. Mummy thinks it's best I just marry someone suitable to get Daddy off my back and"—here he sighs dramatically—"then I can live a neat, but definitely discreet double life."

He explains it so matter-of-factly that my rage of earlier dissipates and I'm overtaken with pity. What kind of life is that? Being denied who you are for the sake of appearances.

"I'm so sorry."

He waves his hands as if shooing away a bothersome fly.

"C'est la vie! From what I hear, you're needing to get your daddy dearest off your tits, as well. So, wanna get married? We'll be the happiest couple, living our separate lives and making each other look good whenever the occasion calls for it. And, if you really want kids, I'm not opposed—that's what in vitro is for. I just can't have sex with you. I'm Golden Gay—never been with a woman and never plan to."

"Ge-rald!" We're both laughing now, so hard that tears are streaming down my face.

"Oh, darling, your mascara!" Gerald leans over, pulls an exquisite silk handkerchief from his pocket, and gently wipes the black streaks from under my eyes.

"This whole situation is so tragic. I don't know if I should laugh or cry."

"You don't have to choose, Miss Evelyn. But come, let's join the rest of the party and drown our sorrows." He extends an arm, gesticulating the way out. "Lead the way."

As we make our way back outside, to the stage of our blind date and the matchmakers in the audience, we are both silent and sobered by the harsh reality check of where we find ourselves at this stage of our lives.

I have never missed Adam more than I do right now.

FIVE

ADAM

WHEN WE GET BACK to Fort Bastion after five nights with the Dutch at Kamp Holland we are informed that our two weeks mid-tour leave is due and we can fly home in the morning. I watch, with a healthy amount of envy, how the lads celebrate the news and immediately start bragging about how they plan to spend the entire time getting pissed and laid, in reverse order of need. Soldiers are notoriously wild, and when they let loose anything goes, and preferably in excess.

I say nothing. I don't know what I'm going home for. I have no clue if Evie will be waiting, ready to make amends, or if she has moved on. It's been four months. Four months of no calls, even though we're allowed to call family once a week via a secure version of Skype. I waited to get a message from her via our comms department that intercepts all emails, but nothing. And I feel physically ill at the thought that, when I get handed my mobile back tomorrow on the plane, that there'll be no good news waiting.

As per army procedure, our flight will stop off in Cyprus for twenty-four hours of R&R and decompression—an all-expenses-paid party. The hotel is barely average, at best, three stars, but there's a beach and the guys are an easy sell on bonfires, barbecues, and free beer. Pretty waitresses, with sexy foreign accents and tanned skin, who offer above-the-belt massages, certainly take care of stress levels before we head home to the very different demands of domestic life.

Pete isn't rejoicing either. When I catch his eye, I give him a nod, and he gets up from his seat and takes a walk with me.

"Everything alright, mate?" I say, lighting a fag.

Pete exhales hard. "Not really. I don' really fancy going back yet, that's all."

"Katja?"

He shoots me a look as if to ask *How do you know?*

"C'mon, we've known each other for a long time, and you've never once looked at a woman like you did Katja."

"That's because I never met anyone who lives in this world and gets it. An' she's beau'iful."

I nod in agreement, slowly letting the smoke in my lungs out in a long exhalation.

"So, use your time off to go see her, or find out if she is due leave. Invite her on a date!"

Pete starts chuckling, a borderline giggle, clearly a bit giddy at the thought.

"So, I jus call her, ask her to take leave and go on a date with me?"

I shrug. "All in, right?"

"Yeah, Paris is neu'ral ground for us—we could meet there."

"Anything is possible if you make it so."

I watch Pete think it over. He's always been a quick, decisive decision-maker, and this time is no different.

"I'm gonna do it. Now I jus have to ask the major for permission to call her. And ask for her number."

I nod.

"And you? What about Evie?"

"I don't know. I hope we can talk things through...if she'll see me. And then there's the cottage, isn't there? Tons of work to keep me busy."

I can see Pete is distracted. "Go! Speak to Cline and get that woman to Paris!"

Pete's smile is broad, his eyes glistening with excitement. The guy has fallen so hard, he has no idea how goofy he looks right now.

"Catch up later, yeah?"

He's already running from me in the direction of the main Ops tent in search of the holy grail that is Katja's contact details.

I'm happy for him. He deserves a good woman.

I just hope mine still wants me.

AFTER A FEW DAYS at the barracks and sleeping in a tiny concrete room on an army cot, I manage to get power and water switched on at the cottage. One of the side extensions, the remnants of a decent-sized utility room off the kitchen, has a basin and metal roof with only a few small holes from being older than I am. I patch it up, followed by a coat of weatherproof paint. I choose the floor of my own house over the base—and that feels kinda good.

In the first week, I reach out to Pete's cousin Phil, who managed to bring in his crew and do the re-thatching of the roof, but it takes longer than I wanted, as all the beams holding up the roof have to be measured, cut, and built before they can lay the thatch. Phil suggests I start working on pouring new concrete for the floors, but that, too, is held up by how long it takes me to clear out the rubble before the actual work can be done. It's back-breaking, and most days my shirt is off by 10 am, with my back in the sun.

It takes me a whole week to find the courage to reach out to Evie. As I feared, she hadn't even listened to my voice note.

I call her mobile a few times in the morning and leave a message. When I don't hear from her by lunchtime, I decide to go round to the house. When I knock, the door is opened by a complete stranger who informs me she bought the house a couple of weeks ago. *She sold the house?* It's then that I decide I need to call her parents. I know her mum likes me enough to at least talk to me. But I'm shit out of luck; on the third ring, her father answers.

"Hello Mr Simpson, it's Adam. I was wondering if—"

"No. She's moved to London, my boy, with her new fella Gerald."

His words slice me so fast that the sting is delayed. "What?" Surely I didn't hear that right?

"Gerald. The architect. She moved with him to London." His words are slow and patronising, like dumbing down a complex subject for the sake of a child.

"I...I just need to speak to her."

"I don't think so."

Rage flares. "You're not the boss of—"

"Bye now."

I STAND with the mobile at my ear, completely deaf to the dialling tone of the terminated call. All at once I'm disorientated, heaving from the shock. My heart has been ripped from my chest and the pain of it brings me to my knees. Literally. Without warning, I empty the contents of my stomach again and again, until I'm dry-retching.

When I finally come to, I turn to look at the cottage. Our cottage. The walls built up, new beams, waiting for the thatch to arrive in the next few days.

I wipe tears from my eyes. It was all for nothing. I should have never left her.

The rest of the day passes in a blur. I walk to the local Co-op to buy a bottle of whatever will numb this pain.

"Do you wan' cola with that? We have a promo on the Jack Daniels at the minute," the girl behind the counter says.

I shake my head and take out my card for tap and pay.

"It's three quid cheaper if you buy it that way," she presses, obviously incredulous that anyone as obviously desperate as I am should pass up on the bargain of the year.

"Sure, darling." I smile to disguise my annoyance. Looking past the milky-bar skin layered with make-up to cover the spots, she is attractive in that small-town way: too much make-up, too few clothes. There's no way those lashes are real.

I make no effort to hide the fact that I'm checking her out.

Her eyes widen and she scurries off to grab the litre of cola. She's back in a flash to ring it up.

"Do you have a rewards card?"

I shoot her a look.

"Never mind, you can use mine."

I watch how she fumbles for the token on a pink, fluffy, pom-pom keychain she pulls from her handbag that's stored under the counter. Her cheeks nearly match the useless furry ball. She bites her bottom lip.

"Fancy sharing this with me?" I ask without thinking.

She smiles a pretty, innocent smile. I'm the big, bad wolf and she's going to Grandma's.

"Sure," she says, "my shift ends in a couple of hours."

I tell her where to find the cottage.

WHEN PENNY The Cashier finds me, I'm already a third deep into the bourbon without having opened the mixer. She arrives bearing a large bottle of cheap cider, and I extrapolate that my new friend isn't much of a drinker.

For lack of a glass or anything else to drink from,

except the single mug I've kept at the cottage, I drain my drink and fill it with the cider.

"Cheers!" We toast a coffee mug to a bourbon bottle.

She giggles. "You don't have a glass!"

I shrug. "It comes in a glass, doesn't it?"

She's cute when she giggles. Long, blonde curls cascade down her shoulders.

"Let's make a bonfire," I announce.

"I loooooove bonfires," she tells me.

I stack the logs in the makeshift firepit, and light the bits of kindling Penny scrounged around for. I'm on my knees, gently blowing at the sparks, coaxing the flames to take.

We make chit-chat while I get the fire going. When I stand up, confident the logs have taken, I find her gaze fixed on me. She pats the space next to her, and I comply by sitting close enough that our arms touch.

"I think military guys are hot," she drops the words into the nighttime. I turn to her, her lips glossy in the glow of the fire. And I notice there's a fine sprinkling of glitter on her eyelids. She leans into me and parts my lips with her tongue; I'm her hesitant flame that needs coaxing to catch fire. Her hand slides up my thigh, but I stop her and pull away.

I start to say that I'm getting over someone, but she shushes me by pressing her lips onto mine. I kiss her back. She tastes of sweet cider and candy-floss lip gloss. I pull her closer, gripping the soft flesh around her hips, and soon her ample breasts are pressed against my chest. She gently pushes me to the ground and straddles me in one smooth movement. From this angle, she is all tits and hips.

"Take off your shirt," I whisper, not trusting my own voice.

She smiles and keeps her eyes firmly on mine when she peels off her sweater. The turquoise bra she removes without prompting. Her breasts are heavy, brown nipples large and taut. I could imagine covering her areola with my mouth, sucking for comfort, if nothing else. I reach for them, curious and mildly aroused. I've never been with anyone except Evie, who is barely a B-cup and whose body is lean and bony in places that usually have flesh.

I squeeze my eyes shut and try to dissolve Evie from my mind.

Penny The Cashier scoots lower down my body. She loosens the button fly of my jeans. She sticks her tongue in my navel and circles the rim of the opening with the tip of her tongue. My cock twitches. Her hand gropes me inside my pants—my cock is only semi-hard—and she grabs it and starts tugging. The sensation confuses me. It should feel amazing, but instead, it just feels okay-ish.

"Stubborn little bastard," she teases and pulls my pants and jeans down in one go, exposing the little bastard to the cold.

Her mouth covers me without further prelude, and I yield, giving Penny The Cashier the motivation to go at it harder. At first, I'm awash with base desire, but the longer I slide in and out of her mouth, the more my brain boycotts this self-destructive act. I retaliate and imagine that Penny The Cashier is Evie, but it's impossible. The uhmmmms and aaaaahs are coming from the wrong mouth.

Everything is all wrong.

"Stop."

Penny The Cashier takes me in deeper. Harder. Faster.

I sit up, pulling away.

"I can't." My voice is flaccid. I hike my trousers up and am on my feet like a jack-in-the-box. Thanks for playing, Penny The Cashier, but the game is over, I think.

She's bewildered.

"Did I do something wrong?" Her lips are engorged with exertion and it makes me cringe.

I pass her abandoned garments to her. "No. I just... can't. I'm sorry. You should go."

I take a long swig from the bottle and relish the burn of the alcohol as it slides down my throat.

Penny The Cashier stalks off, stopping only to take her cheap cider with her. I hear her mutter, "Fucking bastard."

THE WORDS from *Great Expectations* echos in my mind: *"The broken heart. You think you will die, but you just keep living, day after day after terrible day."*

———

THE SUN HAS no mercy and it slaps me awake with his sharp rays the next morning. There's an onslaught of sledgehammers in my head, and there are no curtains to draw. My tongue is stuck to my palate. I reach for the unopened bottle of coke next to me on the mattress, grateful now that Penny The Cashier—*oh God, Penny*—made me buy it. With my thirst momentarily quenched, I fumble, all thumbs, but eventually manage to open my rucksack and find my emergency stash of ibuprofen. The last of the soda washes it down. It's going to be a long-ass day. When my phone rings, I answer, trying my best not to sound too croaky.

"Hello?"

"Mate! How ya doin'?"

"Pete? Yeah, I'm alright. You?"

Pete sounds so ridiculously happy over the phone that it actually aggravates me.

"Did you get to Paris?"

"Katja managed to get some leave, so yeah. But we're in London now, which is why I'm calling. We saw a poster for Evie's exhibition at the Tate Bri'on, and we're going. It's tonight. You'll be there, right?"

When I don't answer, Pete tries again, "I mean, I assume you patched things up? Are you in London right now?" I hear how he switched gears from incredulous to a state of affairs that is more plausible. Of course, I should be in London, supporting the biggest exhibition in my partner's life so far.

"I'm at the cottage in Herefordshire."

"But, you're coming, right?"

"Mate, Evie's moved on, with some guy named Gerald. Who's an architect."

"You serious?"

"Yes."

I hear the muffled conversation between him and Katja before he comes back to talk to me.

"Ka'ja reckons you should come to London anyway. We'll get you a ticket."

I'm staring at my work boots, and start kicking up a patch of moss. "I don't know if that's a good idea."

"You don' just pull the plug on a thirteen-year relationship, Adam," Pete's tone is firm. "You don't just let her go without a figh' mate. At the very least, you owe it to yourself to see with your own eyes that she has moved on and she is happy. Yes?"

I don't answer. Just the thought of seeing Evie with another man makes me want to throw up all over again.

"Yes?" Pete persists.

"Yes."

"Wha' did you just say?"

I clear my throat to make my voice sound more sure than it actually is. "Yes."

"Good. The exhibition opens at half-seven. Wear somethin' nice, okay?"

"Yeah. Hey, Pete, when did you become a fucking relationship guru?"

Pete belts out one of his contagious belly laughs, that reaches me all the way across the invisible telephone lines, and I catch myself half smiling.

"Love, man, it's everything."

Evie

.   .   .

"NO ARTIST SELLS out on the night," I warn him as we're getting dressed for the event.

"Challenge accepted!"

"Seriously, Gerry."

At this point, he finishes the task of tying the bow at the back of my emerald blouse and swings me around, while holding onto my shoulders. His eyes are serious.

"Eve, you're talented and beautiful—all that old money in their vintage Chanels is going to be thrown at you. I'm going to make sure of it."

"Thank you."

"You're perfect and I love you," he tells me for the umpteenth time that day.

"I love you, too."

"Now, let me look at you." He takes a couple of steps back and scans me from head to toe. My hair is shorter now and has been semi-permanently straightened with a Brazilian blow wave, and though I was uncertain about the bangs initially, his advice on my London City Girl Makeover was spot-on. I look good. And despite how Gerald came to be in my life, he has become my best friend in the last few months.

"No, honey, you can't possibly think you can lose your London exhibition virginity in pumps!" He points at my shoes as if I'm wearing dead rats on my feet.

I roll my eyes. "I'll be on my feet all night. I can't wear those nine-inch heels, I'll die!"

"They are Prada, honey, and you cannot go in flats. I forbid it!"

"Fine. I'll wear the kitten heels."

"The Jimmy Choo ones. Not those horrid ones from

M&S." He waves a hand in front of his nose as if he can smell them from the closet in the next room.

"Fine," I grumble, but I stuff the old faithfuls under a scarf in my tote bag when he isn't looking. All at once I feel overwhelmed at the prospect of the exhibition. The excitement of getting this big break is overshadowed by nerves and self-doubt. Any other time Adam would be here to give my outfit a wolf whistle, blind to a potentially poor choice of shoes. He'd draw me into his arms and whisper in my ear, telling me how much he loves me, making me feel like the smartest, most beautiful woman in the room. He has always been that person for me.

I hear Gerry call out as he leaves the apartment, saying he's going to get the car from the garage, and I'm relieved to have a moment alone. Why am I thinking of Adam?

Because he is your *Adam,* my stupid brain reminds me.

My Adam. My Adam was serving on his first tour of Afghanistan when I had my year eleven formal. Even though he pleaded with me to go with someone else so as to not miss the once-in-a-lifetime opportunity, I refused to go without him. So when he came back, he arranged a do-over for me. He roped Mum in to get me a dress, he sent me an invitation along with a corsage, and instructed me to meet him at Wonderland, a popular, if not a bit seedy disco venue within easy reach.

Mum dropped me off, and I remember stepping into the smoky, stale haze, suddenly feeling overdressed and unprepared for a place like that. I scanned the room, all the while, my heart hammering harder and faster in my chest as my anxiety mounted. But at the last moment, Adam seemed to float towards me in a white tuxedo, complete with pink bow tie to match my dress. I'll never forget how he stopped in his tracks and gave me a long, appreciative once-over with his eyes before taking my hands in his and kissing them.

"You're a vision, Evie," he told me, oblivious to the flat, sensible supermarket pumps.

WE DANCED FOR HOURS, until the early hours of the morning, one of the last to leave.

"What's next?" I asked, as we held hands and headed to his barely roadworthy Renault 5 that we dubbed Jason, because it could be a bit of a nightmare to get started.

"Now we watch the sun rise together."

When we got into the car, I recognised the picnic basket on the backseat as being my mum's.

"What's with the—" I asked, pointing at the familiar straw basket.

Adam smiled. "It's our picnic, of course, bespoke made by the best cook in Herefordshire."

"Mum?" I scoffed.

"Yup!" He put the key in the ignition, and we shot each other a look, a mutual prayer to the engine gods that Jason would start the first time. When the engine coughed into life on the first try, we both laughed.

"Now, it's on to Bircher Common so that we can catch the sunrise together." I lifted my hand from the steering wheel for a minute and placed it on my thigh.

"You make me so happy," I said.

"You are my everything, Evie. You deserve so much, and I'm going to make sure you get it."

He was my Adam then. But not anymore.

THE EXHIBITION IS WELL underway and Gerald is working around the room like a pro. He catches my eye and gives me a wink. I smile back. He promised me he'd do all the schmoozing so that I can sell out. Everything seems to be going well, and we're much busier than we thought we'd be. Apparently, last night, there was a sudden surge in ticket sales and that means the gallery is at capacity. I'm still a bundle of nerves, though. We were informed that the Duchess of Cambridge would be "popping by" as she is a patron of the gallery. For security reasons, no one knows what time she'll make her royal appearance, and I know Gerry is going to be hysterical that I didn't warn him.

Someone calls for me, and I see Pete, and a pretty woman on his arm, make their way towards me from the far end of the room and weave through the crowd, smiling and nodding until we embrace and he introduces me to Katja.

I'm still shaking Katja's hand when I get a glimpse of Adam from over her shoulder.

"Adam's here?" I ask Pete, and I'm sure my stomach has just somersaulted.

"Of course," he says coolly. "You know he wou'nt miss it for the world."

"But how did he know?"

Pete shrugs and I see a look pass between him and Katja before Adam is standing right there in front of me.

"Hi," I say, suddenly shy in front of the man I've known almost my whole life.

"Hi."

"You came."

His eyes looked pained, but he nods. "You look...beautiful."

By pure social reflex, I smooth down my new hair. "Thanks."

There's so much to say, but no room to say it. Not here. Not now.

I feel Gerry's hand on the small of my back before he takes initiative and introduces himself to the people of my past now standing before us.

"Adam, yes, I've heard so much about you. How kind of you to come!"

"I've always supported Evie's art." Adam's comeback on the defence totally misses how generic Gerry's words were. And the fact that Gerry is exuding the confidence of a man who isn't threatened is probably going to make Adam even more aggressive. And a fight is the last thing I need tonight.

"Darling"—Gerald leans in to whisper to me—"is it true Kate is coming?"

"Excuse us for a minute," and I pivot Gerry away from Pete and Adam.

"Evie!" Adam grabs my elbow, and I turn to face him.

"Can we talk?" He looks around at the crowd that's getting noisier with every drained glass of complimentary champagne. "Perhaps after?"

I nod. "Yes, we need to." He nods, his expression blank, but I catch a flicker of relief in his eyes. Did he really think I would say no to talking to him?

"Thank you...and congratulations, this series is... exquisite," he tells me, the praise genuine.

I want to say something to lighten the intensity between us, but all I can muster is a "Thank you."

Gerry tugs at me to join a small crowd standing in front of one of my paintings. I lock eyes with Adam in that moment before I allow myself to be dragged away, and all I can think of is how handsome he is and what a damned fool I've been.

Not long after, one of the curators of the gallery comes to find me.

"She's here."

Already there's a stir near the door at the arrival of the duchess. Despite having to stop, shake hands, and greet adoring fans, she manages to glide her way to the centre of the room, where I'm introduced to her, along with the other artists whose work is also on display. It's a surreal moment, and I'm sure I mumbled something nonsensical when she asked me about what inspired my series. I'm still fumbling in front of royalty when an urgent call from the far end of the room interrupts us.

"Duchess! Duchess!"

A woman wearing a hijab is shouting and pushing her way through the crowds, and just as the duchess's security detail steps in front of the covered woman, blocking her path, the woman stops, pulls open the black cloak covering her clothes, and reveals a bomb strapped to her body.

"No one moves!" she shouts.

I'm frozen to the spot, but Adam has appeared out of nowhere and has pushed my head down and pulled me by the arm. Using the crowd as coverage, we're heading towards the back of the room.

The duchess and three of the armed security reach the same doorway leading to the exit route.

"Take her with you," Adam says to one of the security guys and shoves me towards them.

Before he can argue, the duchess intervenes. "Of course," she says and grabs my hand.

"And give me your bulletproof vest and firearm," Adam hisses to the close protection officer. "I'm Staff Sergeant Adam Taylor of 11 EOD and Search Regiment Royal Logistic Corps. If there's anyone here who's seen an IED and can defuse it, it's me."

Everything is happening fast. With a nod from the duchess, one of the security guys stays behind to hand over his gun and vest, while the duchess is being asked to follow one of her men.

I turn to Adam, who is tucking the firearm into the back of his trousers.

"It's going to be okay," he says to me, and amidst the chaos and fear that's palpable in the room, his eyes are calm and steady.

"Adam."

"Trust me, Evie, okay?"

The last thing I see is Adam, ducking down, making his way back through the crowd, carrying the bulletproof vest he should be wearing.

SIX

ADAM

I MANAGE to make my way to Pete, who's crouched down behind a pillar with Katja. Both of them are scanning the room for exits, but it's too late to try to run now; the bomber is at the centre of the room and we are her captives. She's rattling off a speech she has clearly memorised, about the glory of Allah and the evil of the West.

I scan the room quickly; I estimate about two hundred people in the room. The woman closest to me is whimpering and holding her mouth shut to muffle her crying. Almost everyone is on their knees, heads almost touching the ground over the phones calling for help or messaging loved ones. The irony of all of us forced into the prayer position is not lost on me.

I slide Pete the Glock and vest. "Cover me," I instruct and he nods in assent without a word. I see the eyes of the people nearest to us go wide and I put my index finger on my lips.

Our captor has now moved on to the chanting of prayers in Arabic. In our training, we were taught that this indicates that the time of detonation is close. It'll be one of her final prayers before she goes to meet her maker.

I leopard-crawl towards the woman. She's standing with her arms stretched out to the heavens, eyes closed, lost in her chants. I don't get as close as I'd like when she stops and sees me.

"You," she yells, "stop moving!"

I obey but lift my head to make eye contact, and I'm instantly grateful that she isn't wearing a burka. Unlike the burka which covers the whole face with only a small, rectangular, veiled window for the eyes, the hijab is a headscarf that is wrapped around the face, keeping the neck and ears covered. It means I can establish eye contact. It's much harder to kill someone who meets you eye to eye.

I have to be careful. Luring her into talking to me could backfire. She's likely wearing an earpiece that is concealed, and the men behind the attack are giving instructions from a hotel room, or van not too far away. If they hear her talking to me, they'll push her to pull the switch sooner.

"Please, let's talk."

She opens her mouth to answer, but I lift my hand to stop her. And she does. Years of male dominance and oppression mean I have some leeway here. It's a gamble that paid off.

I take another chance and show her both my hands are empty. I keep my eyes fixed on her, and I see I've unsettled her.

"I'm just going to stand up, okay? I just want to talk. I promise I won't come any closer."

She looks around the room to see if she's being ambushed, and I watch her hand on the bomb switch—she's shaking.

"I'm Adam. Please, let these people go. They've done nothing to harm you."

"I am performing the work of Allah, bless his name."

She reverts to Arabic as if answering someone else's question; it's easy to conclude that I was right about her being handled from afar.

From the corner of my eye, I see Pete is close and within range to take a decent shot.

"Does Allah want you to kill all these people?"

"Sacrifices have to be made."

Her resolve is firm and I know I'm running out of time.

"Do you have children? Is your sacrifice worth them growing up without a mother?"

"Allah will reward my family in this life and the next." But a single tear slides down her cheek.

"Please, save yourself, and all of us."

She looks at me, and then I see her lips form a thin line and I know I've lost. There's no way out of this for her. Even if she lets us go, and gets protection from the government, she'll never see her children again and she'll be labelled a traitor with a bounty on her head. She'll be hiding and running her whole life. Death is simpler.

Honourable even. She'll be a dead hero to her children instead of a live traitor.

"It's time."

"Wait! Please, one more prayer for our souls, I beg you."

She smiles. "Yes."

I mimic her stance from earlier—raise my hands to the heavens and close my eyes when she starts the chant, and hope like hell she follows my lead and does the same. I peek after a few seconds and see that she's let go of the switch, and while she hasn't lifted her arms wide, she has her eyes closed, palms face up and open.

Now, Pete! Now!

The moment the shot is fired, I run and leap towards the bomber screaming in agony. The bullet has punched a hole in her thigh, causing her to drop to the ground like a marionette whose strings have been cut.

Pete is by my side in an instant. He's restraining her on the ground and I'm inspecting the bomb. I'm vaguely aware of sirens in the background.

"Stay calm! The police are on their way!" I yell over to the crowd, and I see Katja on her feet, taking control of the mass hysteria erupting as people start the stampede for the doors.

My focus stays on the explosive duck-taped to the woman. With no cutters of any kind, I resort to using my teeth to break the tape strapped over her shoulders. It doesn't work.

"We have to move this device."

"They could have a backup remote detonator," Pete reminds me.

But she's shaking her head between pain-fuelled groans.

"Thank fuck."

"Here." Pete pulls a serrated piece of plastic, that looks like it could be a scalpel, from his pocket.

"Where the hell did you get this?"

Pete shrugs. "Not me'al, not a knife, so the me'al detectors don't pick it up."

"You're a fucking genius." I could kiss the guy.

With the serrated edge of the plastic scalpel, I free the explosives that have been densely packed against her body, careful not to disturb the wires that seem to be hanging by a thread.

"Turn her over. I need to be sure we got everything."

We carefully roll her over onto a shoulder and check her back. It's clean.

"Move it aside and let's get out of here."

By this time, the gallery is empty. I carefully place the bomb out of the way.

Now the woman is hysterical, crying, begging us to finish her.

Both Pete and I ignore her, understanding full well that she could be an important resource for information. No one on our side of the fence would want her dead, not here, not in London. But had this been Afghan? She would have been a goner as soon as we had control of that bomb.

Just then, the bomb unit comes in, heavily clad in protective suits, and we're instructed to step away from the woman. We comply, and before there's time to explain anything, we find ourselves in police cars, heading to the station to give a debrief.

It's going to be a long night.

THE DRIVE DOWN to the police station is a blur. Pete and I are questioned separately, and we provide our contact details and fingerprints as a matter of course. I'm assured that Evie is safe and unharmed. When we are finally able to leave, Pete and I are met with a handful of reporters and flashing cameras, as the news of the attempted bombing must have become public via social media.

Susan Something-or-Other, the police media liaison, prepped us not to speak to the press, and she handles all the questions smoothly. Since the police don't want to reveal the identity of the bomber or whether she's still alive after Pete shot her, we've agreed to do our part in their investigation by not saying anything. We hardly ever talk about our day jobs to anyone outside of our regiment anyway, so it's easy to agree.

Evie

MY ESCAPE with the duchess puts me in a car with her, and she makes polite enquiries into me and my work while her protection officers relay cryptic messages over mobile phones throughout our journey. Her Royal Highness appears cool and calm on the surface, to the point that I start wondering just how often this kind of thing happens to her that she now takes it in her stride. But then I notice that her fingers laced together on her lap are so tense that her knuckles are white. This proof that she's human and probably just as rattled as I am, gives me more comfort than her cool, calm, and collected demeanour. After about ten minutes of driving, I'm asked if there's anywhere safe I'd like to be dropped off.

"Home," I say automatically, but then realise that going back to the apartment where I live with Gerald is not really where I want to be. I want to be with Adam.

"Address?" the driver asks.

"No, wait, could you take me to where Adam is, please?"

The security guards pass a look between each other, and the older one of the two, who oozes an air of seniority and control, gives the other a curt nod.

"Give us a moment," security guard number two says, bringing his phone to his ear. Less than a minute later he has the necessary intel and gives the driver instructions.

"Are you sure you won't be better off with Bert waiting with you?" The duchess offers me one of her men.

"No, thank you, Your Highness. I'll be quite alright by myself," I assure her.

Before I step out of the car, she gives me her hand, and I'm unsure what to do next so I shake it. This makes her smile, and we say goodbye.

I watch the car with the tinted windows drive away, leaving me on the sidewalk opposite the police station where Adam and Pete have been taken for questioning. I rub my bare arms with my hands to smooth away the goosebumps, which I'm not entirely sure are from the cold or the adrenalin of the night's events. I pull out my phone from my clutch bag to see if it's been reported by the news. I scroll through a few headlines, which gives me the shivers all over again.

TERRORIST ATTACK IN THE TATE, ONE SHOT

TERRORIST SHOT IN TATE AFTER FAILED ATTACK

OFF-DUTY SOLDIERS ACT FAST IN ATTEMPTED TATE TERRORIST ATTACK

MY MIND IS REELING with everything that happened, and I keep coming back to Adam and the look in his eyes when he got me to safety before going back to save everyone else. That look. That 'I'm yours and you are mine' look he has only ever had for me since we were kids is still there. We may have gotten lost in lots of ways, navigating adulthood and responsibility, but that look, my feeling of wholeness when he's just in the same room as me, has outlasted everything. And while I don't know what forever looks like, I do know that Adam is the only one who has made me feel completely vulnerable and safe all at once.

When I look up, I see a woman across the street, and I recognise her as Pete's date. I give her a little wave, but then I see her walk towards the entrance of the station where Pete and Adam are exiting. My heart somersaults at the sight of Adam—raw desire for a man I've known and loved most of my life.

ADAM

AS WE LEAVE THE STATION, Pete sees Katja waiting for him. First, we shake hands and he pulls me into a hug.

"We di' alright, Dickens. Thanks, mate."

"Yeah, we did. Thanks for always having my back, man."

"Always." Pete smiles before he walks away and into Katja's embrace.

Just as I'm about to turn and find my way back to a road where I can hail a cabby, I see Evie on the opposite side of the road, her bright green blouse a pop of colour at this misty hour.

I run towards her and pull her into my arms. We kiss and she holds my face in her hands. I never want to let her go again.

"You're okay," I breathe the words onto her lips as our kiss ends.

"Adam, you saved me, you saved all of us."

"Pete helped," I tease.

"Adam, Jesus, don't joke. We could have all been blown up!"

"But we weren't." My eyes are glued to her lips. I want her so badly, but I can't risk scaring her away.

"And I thought you might like meeting the duchess."

She slaps me on the arm and then concedes, "It was the highlight of my night."

I push her away gently. "So, not seeing me then?" It's a joke, but actually I just really need to know where we stand.

Evie leans in to kiss me again, but I don't let her. "You didn't call me," I say softly, my arms still encircling her small waist and I'm relieved she doesn't make any moves to pull away.

"Where are you staying?" she deflects.

"The Holiday Inn Express, on the other side of the river."

"Take me there."

I WANTED TO HAIL A CAB, but Evie insisted we take the bus. Within a few taps on her London transport app, she knew which bus we had to take, and we got lucky getting to the stop just as Number 4 pulled up.

"I would have paid for the cab," I tell her, when she's resting her head on my shoulder, our fingers intertwined. Her hair smells like coconut and her perfume, and it doesn't surprise me. I've seen her spritz perfume in her hair hundreds of times.

"I know." She tilts her head to meet my eyes. "It's just that it's been so long since we rode a bus together in London."

"That weekend in December, just before Christmas, because you wanted to walk in Hyde Park and go to the Christmas market, how many years ago was that?"

"Nine," she tells me without hesitation.

"I still don't understand boiled wine."

We both laugh at the recollection of this memory of me spitting out my first taste of mulled wine. And then a silence that is festered with complications settles between us for most of the bus ride.

"Who's Gerald?"

"Not now. This is our stop." She leads the way off the bus, keeping my hand firmly laced in hers.

We walk fast and when we reach the entrance of the hotel, I stop and make her look at me.

"Evie, stop, wait. Slow down, okay?"

"Why?"

Even though there are so many why's to be answered, everything in me wants to scoop her up and carry her to my room. I want to be as caught up in the moment, but she's with another man.

"I won't make you a cheater, Evie." The words get stuck in my throat. I don't want to say them because I don't want her to walk away.

She kisses me then, hard and full-on. My honour, my resolve to protect hers, is dissolving fast.

"I don't love him, Adam. It's a complicated...arrangement."

I search her face for any evidence that what she's telling me may be untrue. But she's just Evie, my beautiful, perfect love.

"Trust me," she calls on me, just like when I told her to follow the bodyguard out of the building.

And I lead her to my room.

Our lovemaking is fuelled by the vigour of having a close call with death mixed with the tenderness of familiarity and being separated for a long stretch of time. She takes charge, undresses me hastily between kisses, and makes me sit on the edge of the bed. I relish watching her clothes cascade to the floor. Good God, she is sexy.

Then she goes down on her knees in front of me and spreads my knees wide enough apart to accommodate her small frame. I lower my head and capture her lips with my own. My hands start roaming of their own volition: her shoulders, neck, and soft breasts. I get a thrill from pinching the hard nub of her nipples between my thumbs and forefingers, and she rewards me with a husky groan, which fuels my desire for her.

She breaks the kiss, and gently guides my hungry hands from her taut nipples and places them on my thighs. She spreads me a bit wider and then uses her tongue to flick and lick my throbbing cock.

Jesus. Fucking. Christ.

She takes me into her mouth, inch by agonising inch. Her mouth is so wet and warm that I'm sure I'm going to come right then and there. I tell her, but she only lets out a rueful little laugh before taking me in to the hilt. *Ohmygod.*

"I'm so close," I warn her, as I fall back on the bed, surrendering to the pleasure.

She sucks hard and fast, and when I can't stop myself, and push deeper into her perfect, little mouth, she pulls away.

"You vixen!" I groan. "Come here."

And I pull her onto my lap and come up to kiss her. She wraps her legs around me, and my cock grazes her pussy, flicking her clit like a light switch. It's driving us both crazy, and she adjusts herself on my lap, getting my dick deliciously close to her entrance. It takes all my restraint to not just push into her. But I want more.

I pry our bodies loose from each other and lie flat on my back.

"Come here." I pull her onto my torso, and slide under her until my mouth is millimetres from her smooth, swollen lips. I tease her by exhaling my warm breath on her; she bears down onto my mouth. I grab her bum to control her thrusts while my tongue works her pussy.

"Adam, Adam," she repeats my name like a mantra, and I can tell her orgasm is building fast.

"I want you inside me," she begs. "I want to feel you when I come."

She lifts herself off my mouth, and I can't take my eyes off her as she slides onto me. In an instant, I'm on the precipice of losing all control.

She rides me hard and fast, and my hips buck and fall, blissfully in tune with the push and pull. We don't last long and we come together in pants and gasps and groans. I grip her hips with my hands and rock her through the waves and then ripples of our mutual orgasm.

I stay inside her when she rests her head on my chest. My heart is beating so fast, I wait for it to normalise. I run my fingers along her spine, slippery with perspiration. Her body resting on mine feels like home.

"I love you, " I remind her.

We give in to sleep, still lying skin on skin, and some-time in the night, we assume our usual sleeping position where she's the big spoon. Her free arm and leg hug me, and I can feel her cheek pressed against the space between my shoulder blades.

I wake first, with the first signs of daylight, and automatically reach for Evie's hand, which is still supple with sleep and within reach at my torso. I lace my fingers in hers, and she murmurs as she comes to.

I roll over to face her and sweep her hair away from her face.

"Hey."

She smiles a small, sleepy smile. I lean in and kiss her.

"Don't!" She pushes me away. "I haven't cleaned my teeth yet!"

I kiss her again, harder this time, longer. She kisses me back, pressing her breasts into my chest, and I slip a leg between her thighs. When she reaches for me, my cock is already rock hard and hungry for more of her.

"So, you missed me then," she teases, her voice still husky from sleep.

I take the pressure of my thigh off her grinding pussy, and slip a finger inside her. She groans between kisses and holds my bottom lip hostage between her teeth. I drive two fingers into her, in and out, hard and slow, and she gasps and moans, encouraging me to go on. The sound of her pleasure strikes a cord so feral in me, that I soon find myself between her legs.

Afterwards, she lies in the crook of my arm, tracing patterns between the sparse, dark hairs on my chest. Neither of us wants to have the big talk and break this spell of contentment, but I can feel the sense of unease creep in between us. I choose to be the one to rip the Band-Aid.

"You didn't call...and I couldn't get hold of you.

"I changed my number... I needed a fresh start. I was trying to get over you."

"So you sold the house, moved, and changed your number?"

"I did what I needed to, Adam, just like you did what you needed to."

I pull my arm out from under her head and shift away from her.

"So you really didn't want to see me again?" It's a question, not a statement. We both are lying, staring at the ceiling.

"When did you meet Gerald?"

"What does it matter?"

"Do you love him?"

"This is not about Gerald, Adam. This is about us. You. We want different things."

"You want a baby."

She sits up and pulls a crumpled sheet from the bottom of the bed to cover herself. And for a while, she just sits there, but I can see she's thinking hard on what to say next.

"Is it so wrong, so ludicrous, to want to be a mother?"

"No."

"But?"

Now it's my turn to find the right words to say. And there is nothing to say. Although we hardly ever talk about it, we both know that she gave our baby up when we were kids so that we could parent together when we were older. And now we are older.

"But...nothing. If that's what you want. If that's what

you need, let's do it." I sit up and face her. I want her to see how serious I am. "I need you. These last few months have been hell... I...I can't lose you again."

She regards me, tilting her head, and I read the incredulous look in her eyes.

"Why now? Is it because of Gerald? You see me with another man and you go all alpha male on me?" She gives a short, sardonic laugh, cut short by the anger surfacing.

But she's right. When I saw how self-assured Gerald was at her side last night, I went into fight-or-flight mode. I'll do whatever it takes to win her back.

"Jesus!" She scrambles out of bed and starts the search-and-rescue mission of finding her clothes on the floor.

"Evie, please! Can we just talk about this?"

She's pulling on her clothes as if her life depends on it, her voice trembling with rage, "If I had known that all it would take is for me to move in with a guy like Gerald to get you to finally see how important this is to me, I would have done so three years ago!"

"Evie—"

"Don't bloody 'Evie' me!"

I get out of bed, and standing in front of her, I put my hands on her shoulders and still her. She tries to shrug herself free, but I keep her there and wait for her to look up and meet my eyes.

"Hey...hey..."

The rage has given way to tears, and I pull her into my arms and hold her. Almost instantly my naked body responds to hers and I have to work hard to suppress the pressing need.

"We can work this out, okay?"

She pulls back, and the onslaught of vulnerability in her eyes takes my breath away.

"Will you stay and quit the army?"

"Right this minute?"

She waits.

"You know I can't do that. I'd have to at least finish my tour, give notice..."

She shakes her head and steps far out of my embrace.

"I can't be with someone who's gone half the year, sometimes longer. Who could die or be severely injured on any given day. Do you know what it's like to be the one left behind? Dreading the sound of the phone ringing because today might be the day that you get the news that your partner is flying home in a body bag? What kind of life is that for a child?"

"And what kind of life is it for a child to grow up seeing how her grandparents pay for the house and holidays? Where Grandpa's word has more weight than their own father's?"

"What are you saying?"

"I need more time to save up so that I can give you a home, and have a bit to start my own business when I leave the army."

"But I have the money, Adam. We could do all that: buy a new house, and you start a business with the money I made on the old place."

The hope in her voice breaks my heart. She doesn't get it. She comes from an almost perfect family. She doesn't know what it's like to be forced into a family. To always feel like the piece of the jigsaw that doesn't fit. To hide letters from the school inviting you to bring a parent to a sleepover in the school hall because you're not sure your new family really likes you.

I shake my head. "No, Evie, not like that. This is something I need to do. I want my kids to look up to me, to have a father who is worthy to be looked up to. To grow up without a father, without a role model, and without security, makes you feel lost your whole life. I don't want that for my kid. I need to be the one to provide."

"Even if it means losing me?"

"I don't want to lose you. Please wait for me, just a little longer."

Her gaze shifts to the floor, and for a full minute, neither of us says anything. And then she bends to pick up the rest of her clothes and gets dressed.

"I'm sorry. I don't want to wait anymore."

"Evie, please!" I hear my voice tear.

"I have to go; Gerald will be worried."

I pace up to the door and get there before she does. Overcome with rage, I slam my fist into hard metal and wish I felt enough physical pain to not feel as if my heart was being shredded.

"Fuck!" I yell. I see how my knuckles go white and then start oozing blood.

She stops at the door.

"Please don't go," I whisper, hot tears rolling down my face.

She takes my face in her hands and kisses me softly on each cheek. There's so much love in that gesture and so much goodbye that I can't breathe as I watch her close the door behind her.

We changed again, and yet again, and it was now too late and too far to go back, and I went on. And the mists had all solemnly risen now, and the world lay spread before me.

The line from my favourite book ambushed my thoughts, underlining what I already knew. We were over.

There's no thinking after that. I walk straight to the minibar and take out all the bottles of spirits and down them one by one. Then I move onto the small bottles of wine. When the numbness doesn't set in quick enough, I pull on last night's clothes and go in search of a bigger bottle.

SEVEN

ADAM

WITH MY LAST days of leave left, I throw myself into the work at the cottage. A bottle of vodka mixed with orange juice keeps me company all day to make the lonely nights shorter. I pick a dreamless sleep over lying awake, torturing myself with the thought that my life may as well be over. More than once, I think of how stupid I was buying a rundown cottage with the romantic notion that fixing it would solve all my problems.

The day before I have to head back to the airport, back to the sand and sun of my day job, the final section of thatch on the roof goes up. Pete comes round for a 'roof wetting' and we build a makeshift barbecue, from rocks we find at the river, and grill sausages.

"Katja have to go back early?" I ask as I hand him a beer.

Pete nods. "She wan'ed to spend a couple of days wif her family."

"Fair enough."

"I'm going to ask her to marry me," he says with a sheepish grin.

I scan his face to see if he isn't taking the piss, but he's dead serious.

"Congratulations!" I pull him into a bear hug, and when we separate, he digs out a blue, velvet ring box from his pocket.

"You already bought a ring?"

Pete nods, smiles, and drops to one knee, and opens it just like in the movies.

"Oh Jesus!" I can't stop laughing.

"Wait, let me practice!" He clears his throat and we both try to compose ourselves, poker faces on.

"Katja, you are the most beau'iful woman in the world. You're smart, and funny. You are the sunshine I never knew I needed. You make my life worthwhile, and I love you more than I ever knew was possible... Will you marry me?"

An intense silence descends so that all that can be heard are the sausages sizzling over the coals. Pete stays on a bent knee, eyes wide with expectation.

"Nah, I've heard better," I tease.

He snaps the box shut. "You're such an arse, you know that?"

"I'm just kidding, mate. I'm sure she'll say yes. I'm so happy for you."

"Yeah?"

I nod. Pete shoves the box back into his pocket, and I

turn back to the glowing coals and turn the sausages which are now properly cremated on one side.

"What a mess," I mutter.

"Evie?"

"I meant the sausages, but yeah, with Evie, too. In fact, I'd say the sausages are looking great compared to things with Evie." I drain the beer, squash the can, and immediately open another.

Pete's eyes shift from the six-pack to me and then he asks, "Been drownin' your sorrows?"

I shrug. "I'm alright. I'm just...processing."

"What happened?"

I tell him how Evie wants me to quit the army.

"So why don' you?"

I turn to him, and he takes the tongs from me to take over the desecration of the bangers.

"I can't just leave the army, it's my job. What will I do? What jobs are out there for ex-military?"

"General Security. Training and consulting jobs. Private security gigs pay big bucks. When I leave the army, I want to start up my own security firm, hiring ex-army blokes." Pete shoots my feeble excuses down.

"I've considered starting my own business," I confide in him, "but I don't have enough saved for that. So, plan B is I thought I'd wait for a vacancy to open in the training division so that I'll be home more, and the danger is less, before I asked Evie to marry me... I think I'm so close to that now, but it's too late. She's met someone else."

"That guy Gerald?"

I nod, cringing at the thought of him at her side at the gallery.

"He seems too soft for her; it's probably just a rebound."

"I'm not so sure."

I tell him that I have no way of contacting her and that her father refuses to give me her number or tell me where she lives.

"I'll have a go in the morning. Her mum always liked me," Pete offers.

"Thanks, mate."

"But I want something in return."

"Yeah? What?"

Pete gives me a stern look. "The drinking stops tonight."

At that moment I want to deny that the drinking is out of control. But then I think of how I hid all the empty vodka bottles before he arrived, and I have to concede that the self-medicating has to end.

I nod in assent. And that's enough for Pete.

Evie

"WHAT DO you mean he's not looking after himself?" I ask Pete.

I listen to Pete over the phone. He isn't saying much, no solid details out of loyalty to Adam no doubt, but there is so much worry in his voice that I find myself close to hanging up and calling Adam immediately.

I know him. Whether I want to or not. We've been together so long that my knowing him is like a sixth sense, a strand of DNA modified for the sole purpose of knowing him. It's both a blessing and a curse. Finding the perfect gift—blessing. Making it harder to walk away because you understand his struggles are not his fault —curse.

"I don't know what you want me to do?" I tell Pete.

"Tell him you still love him... It's still true, innit?"

"I can't do that. I'm trying to move on." I'm staring out of the window of Gerry's apartment, at a view of the Thames in the hazy distance. Hardly visible because of the London smog.

Pete just about begs me to try again with Adam. He tells me that I'm the strength he needs to stay sober. That Adam wants to be better.

"He doesn't have to be better, Pete. He is..." Here my voice becomes brittle, but I manage to compose myself, before I say, "...He is one of the best people I know. We just want different things, and that has not changed."

I hang up before Pete can repeat his desperate sales pitch because I don't trust myself to hear it again and not reach out to Adam.

ADAM

I GET an email notification from Tate Britain while I'm at the airport. The painting I bought at Evie's exhibition is being shipped, and I'm glad I put down the army-base address for the delivery. It'll be waiting for me when I get back in two months. When I saw it, it was hard not to think that she intended that piece for us—for me. It's a painting of the cottage, the one I just bought. She painted it in a summer setting, the white-washed walls and half-walls partially overgrown with ivy and purple bougainvillaea. The weeping willow tree in the blurry background has an empty swing in it. A charming, abandoned cottage, with a fire-engine-red door.

The only person who could have told her about my purchasing the cottage was Pete, and he wouldn't have. Which means that she added her view of the cottage to her Herefordshire landscape series because she remembered our times there. This little seed of hope is what I'm holding on to.

I'm about to switch my phone off and hand it in to the officer in charge, when I get a text from Pete with Evie's new London address.

You owe me :-)

———————

"WHAT DID HE SAY?" I ask Pete as he strides into the army Rec room. We've been back in Helmand for two days, and Pete's been waiting for an opportunity to get back to Katja.

His face doesn't give away whether his conversation with the major went well or not. He gives gestures with his chin towards the door, and I get up and follow him, pulling a cigarette from my breast pocket.

Only once we are outside, away from the rest, does his face break into a smile.

"He said yes?"

Pete nods. "He said I'd have to wait until we have business with Kamp Holland again, followed by a long speech about him not wasting the taxpayers' hard-earned money on playing cupid blah, blah, blah—but that we were due to go give a day's training there anyway..."

"Brilliant! Do you know when we go?" I say while simultaneously blowing out the smoke of the first, deep, best drag of a fag.

He shakes his head. "Soon I hope. This ring is burnin' a hole in my pocket!"

WHEN WE ARRIVE in Kamp Holland a week later, we are warmly received by the Dutch. Lieutenant Katja Janssen is there, and after we all respectfully greet each other by our ranks, she calls Pete aside to come see the progress on the new maps that have been drawn. I look around to see if any of the others noticed the smiles and looks passed between the two, but the other lads are already following Van der Land to the tent set aside for us for the night.

I see the ring on Katja's finger when she and Pete join the rest of us for dinner. I smile, and she beams back, but I already know that there won't be any announcements. It's hard enough being a woman in the army, but a senior officer in charge of a group of men means that she has to be a soldier first. Her private life will have to remain just that. When Pete takes a seat opposite her, I can see how much restraint he's exercising in not leaning over and touching her.

"It's going to be a long night, buddy," I tease.

"Not long enough," he replies with a wicked grin, and Katja, who must have overheard my comment, flushes bright red.

And then it dawns on me: Pete and I were given a separate tent to the rest of the squad, not as a matter of seniority, but because it would mean no one knows he wouldn't be sleeping in his own cot that night except me.

"You'll take Fosters with you?" He looks over to the German Shepherd who's stretched out on her belly, chin on paws, patiently awaiting her dinner.

"Sure. Cheeky bastard." I chuckle at the canine.

LATER THAT EVENING I find the squad huddled in front of a TV, watching a football game with the Dutch. They are rowdy, and the fact that the game on the TV is England vs the Netherlands is riling everyone up an extra notch.

"Yessssss!" Our boys have jumped out of their seats as England scores its second goal against the Netherlands, making the score 2-2 with five minutes left on the clock.

"You know how this ends, right?" Van der Land sits back in the worn armchair with a smirk dancing on his lips.

"In England, a tie is as good as a win, mate!" announces Alex with only the briefest of glances over his shoulder to a Dutch soldier.

"You do know that this is a replay? The February friendly?"

Before Alex can say another word, the orange shirts

score the winning goal, sealing the losing fate of the English team. A roar of expletives, mixed with joyous laughter from the blokes gathered around the screen fills the room and Van der Land is doubled over, clutching his belly. He's laughing so hard, the only noise he makes is a hiss, hiss, hissing sound.

"Fucking hell!" Alex yells, and there's a bit of commotion from the guys. But in the end, the Dutch offer everyone a beer and they manage to bury the hatchet.

I shake my head at the whole spectacle and call to Fosters to follow me to the tent.

I lie on my cot with the makeshift room to myself and read my tired-looking copy of *Great Expectations* for the umpteenth time. I allowed Fosters to lie at my feet on the cot, but she has scooted right up so that her face is resting on my shoulder. I pat her gently and she seems to doze off.

In a word, I was too cowardly to do what I knew to be right, as I had been too cowardly to avoid doing what I knew to be wrong.

I reread the line and let the book fall to my chest.

I want to write Evie a letter and post it, old-school style. I used to write her a ton of love letters when I left for basic training and she was finishing her A levels. She loved getting them and would write me back, decorating the pages with lipstick kisses and the sweet, floral deodorant she used to wear back then.

If the letters don't work... If this final gesture doesn't break through the barriers keeping us apart... I try not to think any further, and worm out of the canine cuddle and reach for my backpack where I keep a notebook and pen.

THE NEXT MORNING, we get a call, interrupting the training session, to inform us of an incident in Nahr-e Saraj which means we cut our visit short. I call the team together.

"Listen up! We're being choppered to Nahr-e Saraj in thirty minutes—there's some trouble in Llara Kalay. They suspect an IED was planted specifically to hit one of our clinics. There were twenty-three casualties."

"Jesus, why would they hit a clinic?" Young private Devereaux asks, his face ashen. His first tour has hit him hard, and I hope he sees these final weeks don't break him.

"Fucking bastards," Little spits.

"Enough!" I yell, jolting the rest to attention. "Keep your trash talk to yourselves. We have a job to do. Get your gear together."

I watch the guys jog off to their tents, leaving Pete and me.

"I'm sorry our time has been cut short."

"No worries, mission accomplished." Pete can't seem to wipe the goofy grin off his face.

I roll my eyes. "You're making me queasy. Stop being so goddamn happy."

"Sure thing, Dickens."

"Go say goodbye to your girlfriend and let's get out of here."

"Fiancée," he corrects me, before making a dash for the Lieutenant's quarters.

. . .

AFTER THE MEN disperse to gather their gear, I find that my stomach is in knots about Llara Kalay but I try to ignore it. I head to the Lieutenant's tent. Pete and Katja are alone in there. I see them before they see me. Pete is clasping her hands in his, as they stand with their foreheads touching. He's telling her something, but his voice is so low and tender that I can't make out the words. She nods in agreement and smiles before he kisses her.

I take a step back, count to ten, and clear my throat rather loudly before I enter.

"Dickens," Katja greets me.

"Sorry to interrupt, I was wondering if I could ask you to add this to the mailbag?"

"Of course." She takes the envelope from me and places it on her desk, but not before she glances at the address. I see her smile.

"Thank you."

EIGHT

ADAM

NONE of us wants to be going to Nahr-e Saraj. There's an undercurrent of nervous energy on the chopper. I sit back, feigning a nap, but every now and then, I scan my men. I see Pete repack his rucksack, positioning his ammunition closer at hand. Fosters is lying at his feet. Instinctively I slip a hand into my own man bag and feel for the tools I need. I run my fingers along the magazine holding the extra ammo for my close-protection pistol. Silently, I run my fingers over the brass bullets and count the rounds like saying prayers with a rosary.

While Fort Bastion houses around four thousand British troops and a couple of thousand American soldiers, soldiers find comfort in the small-city vibe of the camp. Under all those tunnel tents, there are gyms and coffee shops; hell, there's even a Pizza Hut. Llara Kalay will be the toughest conditions the new guys will have ever experienced besides live combat.

The village in Nahr-e Saraj will offer us nothing more than a spot on the hard, dirt floor in a mud house. It'll be hot and unsanitary, with an outside tap and latrine, if we're lucky. I remind myself to warn the guys that they should think twice before eating and that drinking water out of the tap is off-limits unless you think getting the shits in a place with no flushing toilets is fun.

The helicopter drops us two kilometres outside the village, and we end up marching half the distance before a truck comes to meet us.

"About bloody time!" I bark at the private behind the wheel when I jump in beside him.

"Sorry, sir, but the shit's hit the fan. I'm not actually a driver; he...he had to stay and assist the medic."

"What the hell happened?"

Still fresh in his mind, he spares me none of the gory details of the blast and bloodbath our soldiers have been left to clean up. Of the casualties taken, three of them were British and two American.

"Insurgents?"

He nods. "We've cordoned off the area and cleared the surrounding buildings."

"We'll do a sweep and defuse any other IEDs," I assure him.

"The captain was busy setting up a patrol schedule when I left."

"Our guys will help with the patrol. Take me to him when we get there."

"We're two minutes out, sir."

I put my hand out of the window and slap the metal roof of the vehicle. The squad roars in response. "We're ready," I tell the driver, with more bravado than I feel.

"STAFF SERGEANT ADAM TAYLOR, REPORTING!" I greet the ranking officer in front of me.

"Captain Jeremy King," the captain introduces himself and gestures for me to take a seat on a plastic chair that's seen better days. He sits behind a makeshift desk of wooden planks and trestles. The captain can't be older than forty, but his hair is silver-white. Deep trenches mark his brow.

As he recounts the incident of a few hours earlier, expanding on the facts given to me by Private Reynolds, I listen intently as he tells me that the clinic was set up a month ago to immunise the children and offer pre- and postnatal care to mothers and their infants.

"We've pieced the incident together from a few eyewitnesses. Apparently, there was an empty, plastic coke bottle lying up against the building. One of the children waiting outside kicked it and..."

For a moment we both sit in silence, conjuring an image reel of how the event played out, wishing that we didn't have the ability to imagine it at all. But we can and we do.

"Is there anything else suspicious around, like that coke bottle?"

"No plastic bottles or anything that looks like bombs disguised as rubbish. But there's an old blue Ford Cortina parked a couple of hundred metres away. It hasn't moved for days. My men inspected it and cleared it, but I'd like to have it rechecked by your guys."

"We'll start there. And the patrol—can we help?"

"Yes. We need men to help with the night shift."

"I'll get Sergeant Pete Anderson to pull our men into the rota."

"Good man." He manages a small smile. "That's all for now, Staff."

I take Devereaux and Little with me to search the abandoned vehicle for IEDs, while Pete leads the rest with a wide sweep of the area surrounding the clinic with metal detectors.

Devereaux is the first to approach the car.

"Hey! Whatever you do, don't try and open a door; it may be booby-trapped. The same applies to all the doors and the bonnet."

Peering in through the windows, we see crumpled clothes on the passenger seat, and on the floor behind the driver some rubbish, papers, and coke cans.

"Sir! The key is in the ignition."

"Good work, Little; that means it's booby-trapped, for sure. We're not leaving until we find that bomb, boys."

We run the metal detectors around and underneath the car, and we get the dreaded beep at the left, rear wheel.

"It could be hidden in the hub cap," Devereaux suggests.

"Before we try and take that off, let me check something."

I lie on my back and position myself partially under the vehicle to see what's going on. The adrenaline is pumping and I should be prepared for what's waiting for me, but the spider-like improvised explosive just an inch from my face makes me jolt.

"Fuck," I hiss.

I slide out against the hard, dusty ground.

"It'd be behind the wheel. About the size of my palm. Wires exposed."

I can see Devereaux and Little taking in what I'm telling them.

"It's much smaller than what we're used to seeing."

"Yeah, it doesn't have to be very big if it's positioned right below the fuel tank," Devereaux finishes my assessment for me.

"Can we defuse it manually?"

Little shakes his head. "If it's that small, the work will be delicate. It may be too risky to do manually."

"I agree. I think our best bet is to report it, and get the go-ahead from the captain to blow this baby up. We'd have to clear the area. You guys make sure no civilians come near it. I'll get the go-ahead from King."

"Yes, sir," the duo say in unison, repositioning their AR15s to the front of their bodies, hands ready to aim and shoot.

"Devereaux, have you ever blown up a car before?"

"Only in training, sir."

"Well, today is your lucky day."

Evie

"Well, this is fancy," I whisper to Gerry when we

106

enter the famous Ottolenghi Restaurant at the trendiest address in London.

"It's your birthday, so no expense spared."

Gerry allows the server to pull out my chair for me, waiting for me to be seated before sitting down himself.

I feel out of place here, but I'm distracted by all the sleek minimalist furnishings that are tasteful and expensive. All around us there are Jimmy Choo-, Prada-, and Michael Kors-adorned feet under tables. And I'm relieved that my shoes fit in even if I don't feel like I do.

"You're going to love the citrus salad," Gerry assures me.

Some English Fizz is duly ordered for ten times the price of a good bottle of Prosecco, but I hold my tongue. If there's one thing Gerry does well, it's the lavish life. And it's my birthday.

"To my gorgeous Evelyn"—Gerry raises a glass—"thirty has never looked this good! Here's to you, and a fabulous year to come. May all your dreams come true."

"Thank you." It would be nice to believe him, but here I am, thirty, and what the hell do I have to show for it? One decent exhibition and a bit of money in the bank?

"Come now, don't look so glum. That's such a pedestrian response to a birthday," my companion clucks.

I manage an uninspired smile.

"I just thought...that by now I'd be married...with a baby."

Gerry fakes a yawn. "There's more to life than all that suburbia you're pining after. You're on the road to becoming a very successful *artiste*. You could have fame, money, travel, and men."

"Sounds like the perfect life...for you!"

"True, I'm projecting."

The dishes from the tasting menu start arriving, and the service is so seamless, that I hardly notice one small plate leaving the table and another arriving.

"This is all so lovely,"

"There is more...well if you want there to be?"

The dessert course arrives, and for a few seconds, I'm so absorbed in the theatre of the large, glass cloche being lifted and the smoke ascending like a splendid theatrical curtain to reveal a beautiful arrangement of dollops, smears, foams framing layers of cake and mousse, that I don't see a velvet box being slid across the table.

And then it's there, right in front of me.

I shoot Gerry a look. "Please tell me these are earrings."

My flamboyant friend seemed to have vanished in the puff of dessert smoke, and in front of me is a nervous boy dressed for his part in a stylish, tailored, two-tone, French, cuffed shirt with platinum cufflinks. His non-reply tells me that what's in that box is a key to everything I want for my life, packaged in a neatly veneered facade.

"Gerry..."

He puts up a hand. "Eve, just take a moment and hear me out. This could work. You want to get married. I want to be free of scrutiny. This could work for us. We can live the lives we want on our own terms."

I shake my head. "It's not really about marriage. It's what it means. All the things that come with it. A man who is a lover, a father..."

"Just because Adam sent you a bunch of roses for your birthday, doesn't mean he's going to leave the army for you, Eve."

I hadn't told him that the flowers were from Adam, and I made a point of removing the card, so the fact that he is poking at me with the thorns of Adam's gesture stings. I know his cruelty stems from my rejecting him, so I brush it off. And I keep the knowledge that Adam has never not given me roses for my birthday since forever.

"No. But that doesn't mean I want a fake marriage. Don't you want something real? A life that doesn't mean hiding who you really are?"

He doesn't look at me but smooths invisible creases in the white tablecloth. "So, that's a no?"

"I'm sorry."

Gerry drains his glass without the etiquette I've become accustomed to with him. He replaces his glass on the table with more force than necessary and snatches back the ring box.

"It's a family heirloom, you know. This ring was Ouma's."

"Jesus, Gerry! You asked your parents for the family jewels?"

He considers me then, and there's a plea in his eyes that squeezes my heart so that it hurts to disappoint him.

"I wish I could say yes. I wish I had that kind of grit. But saying yes would mean I've given up on getting a real happily-ever-after."

He nods. "I'm just a boy, Eve, sitting in front of a girl, asking her to marry him...for appearance sake."

We both start laughing, camouflaging the tears we're both trying hard to suppress.

"Well, that's not bloody original at all, is it?" I say.

"Touché," Gerry says with a small smile.

"But, I'll give you points for the reference to one of my favourite movies."

LATER THAT NIGHT, after the third nightcap, and lots of self-pity shots about our circumstances, I fall into bed, still fully dressed. I manage to kick off the heels before I reconstruct a memory in my dreams. In my dream, Adam and I are at the cottage again. We're listening to music on my Discman, sharing the headphones. The song is "Stuck in a Moment" by U2, our favourite band.

"I could be stuck in this moment with you forever," I tell him, twirling a lock of hair around my index finger.

"You don't want that," he says.

I laugh at his ludicrous response. "Of course I do! I love you. I want us to be together forever."

"Your father will never allow it." His voice is flat.

"You don't know that," I say, more assured than I feel, so I add, "Anyway, who I marry will be my decision, not Daddy's. When you ask me, I mean, if you ask me, I'll say yes right away!"

Adam is smiling now, his eyes clear blue like the sky on a cloudless day. "So you think I'll ask you to marry me?"

The blush is instant, and I open my mouth to give him a witty comeback, but he leans in and kisses me full-on. I'm lost in that kiss, the sensation of his tongue in my mouth, the warmth of him penetrating my whole body and travelling to the epicentre of my want. He breaks the kiss, but only to kiss my neck. And then he whispers in my ear, "Marry me..."

I wake up weeping. My mouth is parched and my head is throbbing. I resolve to get up and get water and a headache pill, trying to push the dream of Adam asking me to marry him out of my mind. Because he never did.

NINE

ADAM

EVEN THOUGH I'VE performed a controlled detonation many times before, it certainly pays in thrills and adrenalin being the one to wire the IED up and press the button from a place of safety.

I hand the switch to Devereaux. "She's all yours."

He takes it, his usually pale, worried face alight with excitement. "Are you sure?"

I nod. "Figured I'd better give you something to write home about."

"Lucky bastard!" Little pipes up.

"Okay"—Devereaux smiles—"let's light this baby up!"

"Before you do, run me through all the steps we've taken up to now to ensure the safety of others and ourselves for this controlled explosion."

Devereaux obliges and performs the mental exercise

of going through the necessary steps. I give him the nod, and the three of us put on our ear and eye protection. Little lines up the fire extinguishers.

"Ready whenever you are," I assure Devereaux, who hesitates for just a second before pressing the button.

We blow up the Ford Cortina in a glorious blast: a deep earth-shaking boom followed by a massive balloon of fire and fragments of glass spraying through the air.

It takes us a couple of hours more to put out the flames, and when we head back into the village, the rest of the men are waiting for our food to arrive. I'm not surprised to see a black cast-iron pot in the middle of the floor of our mud hut. It's not the first time we've found ourselves in a remote village where the local women try to express their appreciation for the food parcels and medicine by supplying traditional foods. The spicy aromas are tantalising and torturous to our grumbling bellies. But the food remains untouched for a good reason. Not the least of them being the fear of being poisoned by the enemy. And there's the fact that Brits don't generally handle well with spicy foods and strange meats.

"Has anyone eaten from the pot?" I ask.

A shake of heads all around.

"Good. I don't want any gippo guts. Best wait for the army grub to arrive."

"But isn't it rude not to at least try it?" asks Scottish Dave, the team's larger-than-life Highlander, as big and strong as an ox with an appetite to match.

"Sure, go ahead, but remember you'll end up shitting in a long drop, crying for your mamma, all alone."

"And," Pete adds, "there's no guarantee of TP."

"Aye, my Scottish belly is made of steel!" Dave announces like some gladiator, which incites the rest of the group to egg him on with cries of "Eat it! Eat it! Eat it!"

Pete and I roll our eyes.

"There's always one, isn't there?"

We stand back and watch Scottish Dave open the lid of the pot and take an exaggerated whiff.

"Aromas of spice...cumin...cinnamon..."

More laughter from the lads.

"And what do we have here?" Scottish Dave spears a chunk of meat from the saucy stew with a knife and brings it out of the pot for all of us to see.

"A juicy piece of meat!" He shoves it in his mouth in one go.

"This ends badly," I tell Pete.

"Yeah, someone should have probably warned him that it's probably goat."

"If he's lucky."

When the army grub arrives, it's hotdogs on unbuttered bread rolls with no ketchup. Cans of cola and packets of crisps complete the fare. Scottish Dave tucks into the hotdogs, as well, and not for the first time on this tour, I wonder where the hell he puts it. And for a while, it looks as if he was telling the truth about his gut of steel.

"What the fuck?" Little jumps up from beside Scottish Dave, who just belts out a burp and a laugh in reply.

"Jesus! It smells like you've eaten a dead bloody rat, mate!"

"MacGill!" Pete calls Scottish Dave, "come, you're

with me on the first shift. The rest of you, check out the schedule."

"Walk downwind from that one," I tell Pete as he leaves.

Pete laughs. "It'll take a bit more than a bit of bad wind to off me."

———

THE SOUND of gunfire wakes me. The dialogue of bullets back and forth sounds close by. A second later my brain remembers Pete's foot patrol, and I'm off the dusty floor and on my feet, shouting orders to the guys with me.

We run towards the gunfight, colliding with Captain King's unit.

"Insurgents," I'm informed, "trying to gain entry."

The rebels are persistent bastards, throwing themselves over walls with their fingers on the triggers of their automatic rifles, spraying bullets haphazardly, hoping to hit anyone or anything.

We take cover against the wall of the outer perimeter and do our best sniping at anyone who attempts lunging over the fence.

For a full five minutes, there are no bullets from the enemy. I take a moment to catch my breath, not believing for one second that this is the end. I see Pete emerge from behind a stack of sandbags a few feet away.

"Where's MacGill?" I call out.

"He got the squirts and ran off to find a hole somewhere just before the shit hit the fan!"

"Jesus," I curse to myself. My peripheral vision registers a movement.

"Stay down!" I yell at Pete, swinging left to eliminate the target, who's walking with a sense of calm, waving his rifle around, spraying bullets far and wide. I crouch in the shadow of the wall and fire. My bullet sees the gunman drop to the ground.

"We got him!" I call.

"Medic!" I hear someone yell in the distance and I turn to see Little kneeling beside Pete.

The rest is a blur. I don't know how I got to him, but when the medic arrives, I'm covered in my friend's blood, my hand pressed against the gushing wound in his abdomen.

The medic checks for his pulse, and shakes his head.

"Do something!" I yell.

"Staff, we need to move him—take your hands off him."

"But he'll bleed out."

When no one around me says anything, I drag my eyes over to Pete's face, and it's obvious that no amount of plugging his wound is going to save him. He's already gone.

I remove the pressure of my hands from the hole in Pete. I register that the bleeding has stopped, and intellectually, I understand that's because his heart has stopped beating, but it still won't make sense in my head. I watch my friend being put on a stretcher and being carried away.

"Staff, are you injured?" the medic asks me.

"No."

"Are you sure?" He's shining his torch in my eyes.

I swat him away. Scottish Dave joins the group of men that encircle me, and when I see him I lose it.

"You fucking prick!" I lurch from the ground and push him off his feet. Fuelled by irrational rage, I'm on top of him, beating his face with my fists. I don't know how many punches I get in before I get yanked off of him by the men.

"Walk away!" Captain King instructs me. "Walk away, Dickens."

My eyes slide from MacGill to King and back to MacGill whose face is already swelling. My knuckles start to burn, and I feel everything all at once.

SERGEANT ANDERSON WAS TAKING part in a partnered foot patrol with Afghan National Security Forces to increase security around the village of Llara Kalay, in the Nahr-e Saraj district of Helmand Province.

The patrol had identified insurgents in the area and had begun to search and clear a number of compounds in the village. The Afghan National Army members of the patrol came under fire from insurgents, and the International Security Assistance Force (ISAF) soldiers moved forward to support them. During the fight, Sergeant Anderson was caught in the crossfire and was killed in action.

I REVIEW the official notice of death that will appear on the government website before it gets published. I put my signature on the line that makes it official. So many times in the last forty-eight hours the invisible weight on my chest has made me gasp for air. The pain I feel for losing my friend is physical and acute, yet I can't shed a tear. Tomorrow morning, my friend Sergeant Peter Anderson's body will be flown back to the UK for his burial. Except for a salute as the coffin gets loaded onto the plane, shrouded in the national flag, that will be my farewell to my number two. My brother in battle.

We all know that we could die out here in Afghan, but naively none of us ever believe we'll become one of the tragic statistics.

I'm still lost in my bitterness, wondering what the hell it's all for, and if this life I've chosen is in fact for me, when I get called to the major's office.

"Sir!" I announce myself as I enter.

"Dickens, take a seat."

I do as I'm told, all the while trying to read my superior's face for the reason I've been called in.

"You look like shit."

"Yes, sir."

"What's the problem?"

"I'm not sleeping, sir."

"Go see the doctor when we're done here."

"Yes, sir."

"That's an order," he states, probably knowing full well I won't go anywhere near the medical tent.

I nod.

"I should court-martial you for the assault on MacGill," he continues, "but he came to see me and asked that no charges be made against you. In light of the circumstances and MacGill's request, I've decided to not take the matter further, providing you apologise to him."

"Thank you, Major." I rise from my seat.

"Wait. There's something else."

I sit down again.

"The Queen has sent me a letter, on behalf of the duchess. Little beknown to me, it turns out that not one, but two of my men performed an act of heroism during their leave."

"Yes, sir."

"Now, what I would like to know is, what in God's name were you and Pete doing at an art gallery?"

I crack a smile. "It was Pete's idea that we go to support Evie's exhibition. He..." My throat dries up and my eyeballs feel as if they are on fire. I can't talk about Pete in the past tense; it's too hard.

The major clears his throat. "Well, Staff, I'm delighted to inform you that Her Majesty has bestowed The George Cross to both you and Sergeant Anderson for saving the lives of one hundred and eighty-three Britons and thirty-three tourists."

"Thank you, sir."

The major walks around his desk to shake my hand. "The ceremony will be at Buckingham Palace at the end of the week, so your tour is ending early. You'll leave with the flight going to the UK tomorrow."

"Pete's parents? Will they be at the ceremony?"

"They've been informed."

"Sir, if I may ask, has Sergeant Katja Van der Land of Kamp Holland been informed of Pete's passing?"

"Not by official channels. That's up to the family."

"Then I'd like to make that call, please."

The major nods. "You're a good man, Staff."

I wait until the catering tent starts serving supper, then I head straight to the drinks stand and get my two-beer quota for the day. Since I'm the first one there, and there's no one behind me in the line, I lean in to the officer in charge of rationing.

"Any chance I can have my mate Pete's quota, too?"

"I don't think so, Staff."

"Please," I plead, shamelessly exploiting my dead friend for a drink.

"Fine," he gives in, but not before checking who may have been watching.

I grab the four beers, shoving two of them up my sleeve, and don't look back.

I guzzle the first two lagers in a hurry, and after crushing the cans, and hiding the other two, each in one boot from two spare pairs, I head to the comms tent to make the call to Katja.

When I get her on the line, I can hear the smile in her voice as she greets me in the formal way I expect. Maybe she thought this was a follow-up call on the training we had to cut short. So much can change in a matter of thirty-six hours. You can fly in a chopper, your boss can volunteer you and your team for foot patrol, and then you can get shot and die.

"Staff, are you there?"

"I'm here...sorry. Lieuten— Katja...it's Pete."

"Is he okay? Was he injured?"

I clear my throat. "No...I mean yes. He was shot on a foot patrol and...died."

"Oh, my God." The words are barely a whisper.

"I'm so so sorry."

"I don't know what to say...what? He's dead?"

"I'm so sorry. He's being flown home in the morning. If you give me your number, I can get in touch about the...funeral."

At the word "funeral," I hear her break, and a sob smothers the line.

"I'm so sorry."

For a long while, she cries into the phone, and I just sit and listen.

Evie

DEAR EVIE,

We've been sent to Kamp Holland to provide some explosives training. Pete has wasted no time and asked Katja to marry him. The guy is so love-struck it's quite nauseating. But they are good together.

Like us...like we could be...or should be...?

Growing up, never having seen what love between a man and a woman can be, I never bought into the idea of soul mates. I fancied a few girls at school before I met you, but none of them made me want to be better.

And then you came along. With your wild red hair, shy smile, and you liked me, for who I was. It was the first time in my life I didn't have to "be good" or pretend for approval or affection. I still don't know what you saw in me back then, but I want you to know that I have lived every day since I realised I loved you, trying to be the man you saw in me...

When I saw you in London, I never got the chance to tell you that I bought our cottage. You know, the one we used to go to, to get away from your parent's open-door policy. Pete got me onto buying a place to fix up, and when I found the cottage for sale, I bought it for next to nothing. I'm fixing it up and it's coming along—managed to lay new cement for the floors and Pete's cousin did new thatch for the roof. I'd really like to show it to you. Do you want to come and see it?

I won't lie, seeing you at the exhibition with another man at your side made me sick to my stomach. It should have been me there with you, celebrating your big break and success. I messed up what we had, Evie, I knew that then, but when I saw you with Gerald... I guess, I didn't believe you'd move on so fast...but then it had been nearly four months, and as you have told me many times before— your life doesn't come to standstill when I go on tour.

I get that now. I have two weeks left before the tour ends. Can we talk, please? I want to make things work.

Please tell me it isn't too late.

I love you.

Always yours,

Adam

P.S. Happy Birthday

I READ and reread the letter, wondering why the hell now he chooses to write to me when he hasn't penned me a letter since his days in basic training. Trying to take my mind off the seconds ticking away, I pace the length of the bathroom and think of Adam buying the cottage—the one I captured as a derelict, crumbling building as part of my Herefordshire Landscape Series. I'd love to see how he has redone it. My painting may be one of the last images of the abandoned house, and now it's sold and likely hanging in a wallpapered living room somewhere.

Why was the letter waiting for me today of all days?

The timer on my mobile beeps, indicating the three-minute waiting period is over. I squeeze my eyes shut and take a deep breath before I dare look at the oval window of the pregnancy-test stick.

Even though I know that two lines mean it's positive, that I'm pregnant, I double-check the instruction leaflet because I can't believe it.

The two, solid, blue lines stay in place, no matter how many times I blink, and slowly my brain catches up to reality, not that I'm pregnant, but that I'm going to have a baby. Things may not be ideal, but I'm not some scared teenager this time. I can do it alone if I have to—and there's no question that I do want this baby.

There's a knock on the bathroom door. "Evie, darling. Would you like a glass of wine?"

It's Gerry. I flush the loo for the sake of appearances and stuff the pregnancy test in the pocket of my jumper, before I open the door, trying to be casual. "Not tonight. But tell me all about your blind date with the personal trainer slash model."

TWO WEEKS LATER, another letter from Adam arrives, and this time I recognise the postmarks immediately. The thrill of receiving personal mail, has me smiling as I rip open the envelope and pull out a single sheet of paper. If Adam's last letter wasn't a once-off, and he's choosing to write to me regularly, that means he's thinking about me. Us. This is good, I tell myself, and decide to make a cup of tea before I sit down and read it.

DEAR EVIE,

I intended to fill this letter with all the visions and dreams we had for our future. The ones we sat and sketched out while we walked hand in hand from school... or when we'd lie under the willow tree at the cottage. Do you remember those days?

I miss them. I miss seeing the world as a place of possibilities. I miss you.

I always miss you, even if I don't say it. You're on my mind on the quiet days between missions, and even when I'm brushing away the sand, holding my breath, staring at an explosive, it's you I see in my mind's eye that second before I clip the wires. I need you to know that.

Pete got shot. He was on patrol when insurgents infiltrated the village. I'm sorry to let you know that he didn't survive. I just got the news today that I'm allowed to go home tomorrow so that I can receive The George Cross for that night at your exhibition. Pete's parents will receive his medal on his behalf...and there'll be the funeral. I can't imagine that they'll find any comfort in a bit of silver and

gold. I made the call to Katja myself. It was one of the
hardest things I've ever had to do.

He was my best mate...and now he is gone.

I know he was your friend, too, and I'm sorry for your
loss, my love.

Adam

I FOLD the letter and let the tears come. Gerry finds me
on the sofa in the semi-darkness when he comes home
from work. I have no idea how long I've been sitting in
the corner of the sofa with my legs tucked in beneath me.
But my tea is cold, and my face is wet.

"Sweetie, what's the matter?"

When I start sobbing because the words are too
heavy to speak, Gerry pulls me into his arms.

"Adam?"

I shake my head and hand him the letter. He reaches
for the switch of the lamp on the side table and then
scans the single sheet of paper, and Adam's boyish scrawl.

"Oh, honey." And pulls me back into his arms, and
strokes my hair as I cry even harder. All I keep thinking
is, what if it had been Adam—it could have been him, and
then, and then...the baby...

"Come, let's open a bottle of Sangiovese and drown
our sorrows."

I shake my head. "I'm...not feeling very well. I think
I'll climb into bed and have an early night."

Gerry considers me with a single raised brow.

"I haven't been feeling very well for the last few days.

I have an appointment with the GP for tomorrow," I add as I avert my gaze. At least the last part is true.

"Okay, then. Let me bring you a fresh cup."

Relieved, I get up to change into my PJs. I feel guilty for not letting him in on my pregnancy. But as good a friend as he is, it doesn't feel right to tell him, or anyone else before I've spoken to Adam.

I allow Gerry to fuss over me when he comes into my room with tea, biscuits, and a hot-water bottle. Once he leaves, I take out my phone and text Adam asking him to let me know when Pete's funeral will be—knowing full well that by doing so, I've given him my new number and opened the lines of direct communication again.

I'm not 100 percent sure that I'm doing the right thing by potentially going down this road with Adam again, but...life's short, and at the very least, he needs to know he's going to be a dad.

TEN

ADAM

I TAKE up my position amongst Pete's two brothers and his father, and help carry the coffin out of the church to the plot prepared in the cemetery, on the grounds. More than once, I find myself squeezing my eyes shut, trying not to think about the fact that my mate's body is in this wooden box and that the box is going to be six feet under within the hour.

It breaks my heart to see Katja standing up front with the family at the graveside—out of place, to one side. The worst kind of alone: alone but not alone. There aren't enough arms and shoulders amongst the family to go around, and so I go and stand beside her and take her hand. She squeezes it without taking her eyes off the polished pine box that is suspended above a hole in the ground. I hold her hand and don't let go until I walk with her to the cavity and she drops a single-stem red rose onto the coffin. Only then does she turn to me and crumple into my arms. My coat absorbs her tears and the sound of her sobs, but no matter how tightly I hold her, she cannot stop shaking.

"He loved you so much," I tell her over and over again. When she does look up, the tip of her nose is red and her blue eyes look like they're set on soft, pink cushions. She pulls a used tissue from her pocket and dabs her nose.

"He loved you, too, you know? He never shut up about you." She tells me and a laugh shoulders its way through the pain.

"He was my best friend," I murmur, not trusting my own voice.

She looks back at the grave and then back at me. "I'm not sure I'm going to stay in the army," she tells me. "I want...to live. Really live, you know?"

I do know. I nod. Then and there, the realisation hits me that I'm not sure I want to go back to military life either. It's an old cliché of life being too short but if you live it well, it's long enough. I'm desperate to be in the latter category, to be living my best life so that when I die there are few regrets. That life has to have Evie in it.

THERE ARE SO many people at Pete's funeral that it isn't until the coffin is lowered into the grave, and half the people have wandered off, making their way to the local Presbytarian church hall for refreshments, that I see Evie standing in a puddle of autumn leaves under an oak tree.

She's wrapped in a long, black overcoat against the chill in the air.

I walk up to her. It's been two and half months since I last saw her that night at the exhibition...the night we went back to my hotel room and the getting-back-together sex turned into another break-up. The same fight on rinse and repeat. I walk in big strides to meet her, eager to see her up close, to hold her again. If she'll let me.

But I don't have to worry about that for long. Her arms are outstretched to receive me before I reach her. And it's here, in her embrace, that I find the place I need to release the tears I've been holding back.

"I'm so sorry," she soothes me like a child. Every time I try to take control of the outpour, the tears just come harder, until eventually, I lose track of everything. Time. Place. The people around us. It all dissolves as I purge the ugly mess that is my grief.

"Let's go somewhere to talk," I say when eventually my head is thick and I feel the onset of dehydration. "There's a tea room just a short walk from here."

She agrees, and I take her hand and lead the way. We stay joined like this. She's the first to let go when we step inside the frilly, floral shop. It reminds me of what I imagine a granny's house must look like: white wicker tables and chairs, adorned with a pastel palette of flower-patterned cushions and matching tablecloths with double-layered frills.

Evie wriggles out of her coat so that it lands perfectly hung over the back of the chair. The sight of her is like a healing balm for my splintered soul. Her porcelain face is faintly flushed by the cold, and I think she looks more radiant and content than I've seen her in years.

A sinking feeling settles in my gut. *Does this mean that she and Gerald...? Is Gerald the reason she's so happy?*

"Are you alright?" she asks me just as the tray with the tea arrives. To avoid her searching eyes, I set my focus on the pouring of the milk, adding the sugar, and then finally adding the tea to the dainty cups at the very end.

She smiles. "I've nearly forgotten how pedantic you can be about tea."

I know she means it as a compliment, but the fact that she's forgotten this aspect about me is an unconsciously cruel slap. I slide the cup and saucer across to her, then I retrieve the small hip flask from my coat pocket and add a generous splash of whiskey to my cup.

"What's this?" Her eyes are wide. But instead of answering her, I down the tea in one go.

"Adam! What the hell?" she hisses.

I shake my head slowly and suck the air between my teeth to counter the burn rolling down my throat.

"I'm fine."

"How the hell can you say you're fine?!"

I can't meet her eyes. I'm ashamed for this sham of a man I've become.

She reaches across the table and puts a hand on my arm.

"Adam, when last have you slept?"

I can't answer her. The last few days have been a blur and it feels like every time I shut my eyes, I hear the shot and then have Pete in my arms, bleeding out.

"I'm okay," I tell her.

130

"Fine. Then I'm leaving."

Evie

"EVIE, WAIT!"

Adam is following me down the street as I make a beeline to my car.

"Please, wait." He's caught up with me and taken hold of my arm. I shake him off and carry on walking. Faster. I've always known that Adam was prone to self-destruction. This and the risks of his job have kept me awake many a night. But to see him give himself over to drink tears my heart to shreds. He doesn't know about Pete's call. He doesn't know that Pete saw the signs and was so worried that he reached out to me to tell me that he saw the empty vodka bottles hidden away. That he'd spoken to him and that Adam had agreed to get it under control. And maybe he did. But clearly Pete's death had made him turn to the booze again.

Emotions I had longtime buried, feelings I thought we'd both worked through, hit me like a tsunami. The day he went with me to the abortion clinic, just weeks before his second tour. We'd both decided it was the right decision. We were too young. Not ready. And we'd have plenty of time in the future to have a family. Also, my parents would have flipped. I remember being scared, like I am today. Alone on the steel table, while the procedure was being done, I was disconnected from the life growing inside me. I was just a child myself, for God's sake. But this is different. I want this baby. I want it with Adam, but not like this.

"I'm not letting you walk away from me this time," he says as he synchronises his strides with my own. The faint smell of whiskey on his breath makes me want to scream. How dare he ruin himself like this? Now, when I need him most!

"Stop. Just stop," I say. I catch my breath, and pressure on my bladder makes me wish I'd used the tea-house facility before storming out.

Now we're in the middle of the sidewalk, staring each other down. His cheeks seem drawn, more than usual after a tour. The lines on his forehead are more pronounced. My concern for him is instinctive, and any other time, I'd be consoling him. Nurturing him off the booze and cigarettes. But not this time. I have the baby to worry about.

"That wasn't your first drink today, was it?"

Adam kicks at an imaginary stone and can't look me in the face.

"I can't do this."

"It's just temporary... I just needed...something."

We both know he means *someone*.

I shake my head. I can't do this now. Something's wrong. I feel as if I've wet myself. I open my coat to see if I've involuntarily peed myself and see an alarming red patch of blood spreading between my legs.

"Jesus, Evie, you're bleeding!"

Adam is holding me up, keeping me on my feet as I feel my legs give way.

"Take me to a hospital. I think I'm losing the baby."

ELEVEN

ADAM

EVIE IS HYPERVENTILATING before my eyes. She rummages through her handbag and thrusts her car keys into my hands. My brain is still trying to play catch up.

I'm losing the...baby?

She's pregnant?

I'm still processing the fact that the woman I love, have loved all of my adult life, is having a baby...losing a baby...and it could be mine. Flashbacks to the night in my hotel room play like a movie reel on fast forward in my head. These thoughts are fleeting, and I'm in full-on crisis mode, getting Evie into the car and then running around to get in myself.

It's only once I'm behind the wheel that I realise I'm legally not permitted to drive.

"Shit!" I slam my open palms against the steering wheel.

"Drive! There's too much blood...oh God!" She groans.

I turn her shoulders to face me. I need both of us to just take a moment before I take the risk of driving illegally. I already know I have to. I hate myself for being in this situation, for being the drunk.

"Evie, I need you to take a long, deep breath for me, okay?"

Her eyes are wide and wild with fear like I've never seen them before. But she tries—she closes her eyes and inhales. On the exhale, she starts shaking and the tears come.

"Okay, here we go. Everything's going to be alright."

I turn the key in the ignition and pray like fuck that I get Evie to the hospital in time and that I don't get pulled over in the process.

"All you have to do is breathe. Can you do that for me?"

She nods. Her forced inhalations and exhalations soon become rhythmic. It's the longest twenty minutes of my life getting her to the hospital. When the rushed but organised chaos of admissions at the A&E are done and she's lying on a gurney behind a faded blue curtain, I sit beside her, holding her hand. The consultant is taking forever to get to us.

"Evie..." Somehow the words, the question I want to ask just won't come. I'm petrified that the answer might be no. I'm scared that the answer may well be yes.

She nods and squeezes my hand.

"The baby is mine?"

"Yes," she whispers and I see how her eyes well up again.

"Jesus." I let go of her hand and run my fingers through my hair. Evie is pregnant. With my child. I'm going to be a father. But then I glance over at the bloody mess in her lap, and I see it all being ripped away from us.

I'm a fucking mess.

"I get it. You're not ready. I'm not asking you to..."

"What? What are you saying?"

The curtain gets pulled back, and a consultant steps in and introduces himself without eye contact and an inaudible mumble.

"Hey, do you think you can at least look at us when you speak?" I stand, and just to make sure he heard me, I take a step forward.

"Adam!" Evie tries to talk me down, but there's no use.

"You're the father?" the weedy consultant asks, with a tone laced with accusation.

"No," Evie interjects, "he's just a friend."

I turn to her. *What?*

"No, I'm the baby's father," I bark at the consultant.

"I'm going to have to ask you to leave," the white coat threatens me.

I take another step forward. "Excuse me?"

The consultant doesn't back down. "Have you been drinking, sir?"

I freeze.

"He was just leaving," Evie reassures the consultant. And for the second time in mere minutes, I find myself turning to her with *What?* written all over my face. But there's no mistake reading her eyes. She wants me to go.

I ignore the look of satisfaction on his smug face and leave the room to wait outside the building and sober up.

I LOSE TRACK OF TIME. I make countless trips to the hospital shop for coffee, and when I smoke the last cigarette in the packet, I buy gum. I've sent Evie numerous texts, asking how she is, but she hasn't replied.

The seats in the general waiting area are uncomfortable and designed to make you lose the will to live, and I'm finding it hard enough to sit still as the caffeine jitters set in on top of a helluva hangover. I end up pacing. Thirty-two paces up and down the corridor.

And then I see Gerald pass, and I run to catch up to him.

"Hey!"

He swings around and flicks his golden fringe out of his eyes. He's shorter than I remember.

When he recognises me, he dismisses me at once. "Not now."

Well, fuck. That. Shit.

I grab him by the shoulder, and rotate him to face me like a ballerina in a girl's jewellery box, dancing in the wrong direction.

Despite my roughness, Gerald is unperturbed. "What?"

"How is she?" I let go of him and I feel the surge of aggression being replaced with worry.

"I've come to take her to her parents."

"But is she okay? The…"

He sighs, and steers me to a chair, makes me sit down, and then perches on the edge of a chair next to mine and faces me.

"Listen to me. If you want to have a hope of being part of your baby's life, you're going to have to step up. Eve loves you, but she can and will live without you if she thinks you won't be a good influence on the baby. So I suggest you leave now, think hard about what you want from your life—the army or Evie—and do what you have to do." He looks me over, and I can tell he knows I was drunk just a couple of hours ago, whether he can see it on me, or if Evie told him the details from earlier, I'm not sure. Nevertheless, he does me the courtesy of not mentioning the booze.

My head is suddenly heavy and it hangs with shame. I cover my face with my hands and press my palms against my eye sockets until I see stars. To my surprise, Gerald waits for me to look up.

"You're a good man. A good friend. I can see why Evie is with you."

Gerald shakes his head and stands up. "Eve and I were never together. We share a flat in London. I asked her to marry me on her birthday. She said no."

"She said no?"

"I'm gay. Look, I have to go. I'm here as her friend, and right now she could really do with one of those. I've said as much as I can. You kids are going to have to sort things out for yourselves."

My mind is reeling with everything Gerald has told me.

"Please, please just tell her I love her."

He nods.

I watch the man I've despised for no real reason walk down the hallway to the room I want to be in. To be everything the woman I love needs right now. And it feels like my whole life has just exploded and all the tiny bits that make up me have shattered into tiny splinters, making it impossible to put me together again.

"Love her, love her, love her! If she favours you, love her. If she wounds you, love her. If she tears your heart to pieces—and as it gets older and stronger, it will tear deeper —love her, love her, love her!" - Charles Dickens, Great Expectations

Evie

MUM KNOCKS SOFTLY on the door before she wheels the wooden tea trolley into the room. This is my gilded cage. Under my mother's wing, I have to try to keep the hatchling inside me alive.

"Thought you might want a cuppa," Mum offers, and starts pouring the orangey-brown liquid into a mug. Then the milk. Then the sugar. I hold my tongue, not wanting to detract from her gesture by telling her she's making it all wrong.

"Three days down, and seven to go," Mum says cheerfully, "Biccie?"

I shake my head. Ever since the bleed, I've lost my appetite. I was discharged the same day, once the bleeding had stopped for four consecutive hours. The ultrasound showed that my cervix had spontaneously dilated. But all I saw on the small, black monitor, was a lopsided grey kidney bean with a sprouting of limbs. And I heard the heartbeat. That was enough for me to listen to the doctor's advice and stay on bed rest for ten days, and after a follow-up, the doctor might decide to stitch me closed, if nature hasn't worked her magic.

"You should eat," Mum says, sitting on the edge of the bed.

"I will...a bit later," I assure her, taking a slow sip of the tea which tastes nothing like Adam's. It's too sweet and too weak, and I'm certain there wasn't even a teapot in the vicinity of this cup being made.

"Your father and I were talking last night...about your...situation, and we both think it's best if you reconcile with Adam."

My parents are so old-fashioned I could laugh. But instead, I find myself overwhelmed with a vast and endless sense of loss and feeling alone. I shake my head.

"No, Mum. That chapter is closed. You and Dad were right. Adam can't be the man I need."

"But there's a baby to consider now, Eve. You have to think of that. And you and Gerald...?"

I scoff. "Gerald is a good friend, but nothing more. I'm thinking of the baby and myself. I can manage."

Mum gives my words time to settle.

"Well...you could stay here. We could convert one of the spare rooms into a nursery, and of course, you can have the loft to work in?"

I dismiss the idea immediately, but I don't want to

hurt Mum's feelings. I know that even though the pregnancy has come as a shock to her, she's overjoyed at the
thought of finally joining the Nanny Club amongst her
friends.

"I'll think about it."

"I'm hoping for a girl," she confides in me, and there's
unfiltered delight in the way her lips curl into a quiet
smile.

"And Daddy?"

Mum sighs. "You know your father, he takes a while
to warm up. But he will. You'll see. He was already
talking about setting up a small savings account for the
little one."

I nod, but deep down, I know how much disappointment I must have caused. A baby out of wedlock was
definitely not part of the perfect-daughter picture either
of my parents has had of me. I've carried around, being
the only child, like a scarf that's a compulsory uniform.
Some days it's a perfect fit with the mood, but other
times, it's simply a noose around my neck, causing me to
gasp for air.

"I'm feeling a little tired, Mum, do you mind...?"

"Of course."

She hovers over me and plants a kiss on my forehead,
something she hasn't done since I was a little girl.

"I'm going to be okay, Mum."

She nods, and I watch her wheel the trolley out, the
plate of biscuits untouched.

It's not until she closes the door behind her, that I
open my mobile to check my email. I applied for a temporary position in a gallery in Belgium, something to tide

me over until the baby is born. When I saw the advertisement for a gallery manager, I imagined that putting some real distance between myself and Adam, and even from Mum and Dad is just what I need.

I refresh my email, squeeze my eyes shut, and hold my breath in hope that the universe agrees with me, and that there'll be an email saying I at least got an interview.

I open my right eye and can hardly believe that I do, in fact, have a response from the gallery. I open the mail and scan it quickly. They'd like to schedule a telephone interview for three days from now. I immediately reply, thanking them and confirming the date and time. Then I lean back in bed and place a hand on my belly.

"We're going to be okay, little one. It might just be you and me, kiddo. But I promise you, we will be okay."

TWELVE

ADAM

I'M NOT sure I can do this.

I'm standing in front of the door of my officer in charge, and I know that the first thing I need to do is knock. Enter. State my intention to resign. Ask for help.

Over the years I've seen other soldiers start the downward spiral. And it isn't only triggered by a single traumatic episode. It can be years and years of accumulative horror that eventually takes hold of them like a malicious cancer. It ravages their minds, bodies, and in the end, swallows their lives and everything they love—whole. The sights and sounds you've experienced in a war zone, stay with you, destroying any kind of peace, even when you're home, safe and sound.

I've learned nothing from seeing it happen before. I'm no stronger than men before me who have given up on themselves. Not smarter. The temporary solace at the bottom of the bottle is now an unquenchable thirst that I have to sate as if my life depends on it.

Evie was right about everything. The drinking. My inadequacy as a man who's going to be a father.

I wipe the clamminess off my hands and onto my trousers. I draw a shaky breath and knock on the door. I take the first step.

———

THE WEEKS that follow are the hardest of my life. I'm granted a leave of absence to start an out-patient recovery programme for the booze, and I have to attend two group and one one-on-one therapy sessions per week. I'm still smoking, which is shit, but my therapist has assured me that tackling the drinking and trauma is enough for now.

I keep busy. After laying the floors throughout the cottage, I move on to installing double-glazed windows. The work is physical enough to help me sleep at night, and requires plenty of accuracy to keep me focused.

I clean the paint splats from my hands with an old rag and turpentine before heading out to the Co-op in the late afternoon. This is part of my new routine—to pick up a few bits for dinner every evening. I outbid someone on eBay for a vintage cooker and oven, which I installed in the kitchen, and most days I cook a simple stir-fry of meat and veg. I haven't seen Penny The Cashier since that night. In the unforgiving daylight of sobriety, I'm ashamed of the whole incident.

Step 8: I've made a list of all persons I have harmed, and am willing to make amends to them all.

My phone rings while I stroll to the shop. Instinctively. I hope that it'll be Evie. A month has passed since I saw her in the hospital. I text her every day, first thing in the morning, and remind her that I love her. I want her to know that she'll always be my first waking thought. I can see that she reads the messages, but until now, she hasn't replied.

When I answer, it's Second Lieutenant Wilson from the Human Resources Department.

"Staff, are you well?"

"I'm getting there."

"That's good to hear." I hear the shift from brief small talk to the real reason she's calling.

"The reason for my call is personal. I hope that's okay?" She doesn't wait for a reply. "I want to ask if you'd be interested in adopting Fosters. You know, the German shepherd that Sergeant Anderson handled?"

Fosters is one of Pete's dogs, the German shepherd that travelled with us in Afghan on the last tour.

"But Fosters belongs to the army?"

"Well, yes. But she recently got injured, and she isn't fit for duty anymore. We'd like to rehome her instead of..."

"What do you mean she isn't fit for duty? What's happened?"

"She lost a leg in a blast. Front left. She's on the mend after her surgery, and otherwise healthy, and will able to get around just fine as a pet. Do you want to come and see her? I can have her transported to the Herefordshire base for you."

"I don't know..." I don't tell her that I'm barely

keeping myself together. I'm not sure I'm ready for the responsibility of a cactus let alone a dog.

"We just thought, since Sergeant Anderson was your friend, you might consider it? If not, that's fine, too." She says it matter-of-factly, a bit too business-like, which makes me think she's compensating for her disappointment in my hesitation.

"Can I think about it?"

"Of course, but I need to know by Friday."

As much I want to take Fosters on to honour my best mate, I'm painfully aware of how many bad decisions I've made recently. And I don't want to make another, so I do what I know I should: I decide to talk it through with my sponsor and therapist.

I make a case for the dog. Poor Fosters—lost her handler and a limb and now is in the orphanage for throwaway dogs.

Then I make a case for myself. I don't think I can take her, but I know I can't leave her rehoming to fate. The irony of an alcoholic adopting a dog named after a beer seems to fit my life just right.

Expecting both my current mentors to dismiss the idea out of hand, I'm taken aback when they both independently agree that my adopting Pete's dog would be good for me. I find myself elated that these men both believe I'm ready to be responsible for something more than just myself. It feels like real progress and I'm on a high for the next few days, while I shop for all the extra things I'll need for my dog. I call Lieutenant Wilson and tell her the news, and we arrange that I collect Fosters on Friday.

. . .

SECOND LIEUTENANT MARIANNE WILSON'S face breaks into a wide smile when I knock on her door. I salute her even though I'm in my civvies.

"I'm so glad you're taking her, Staff; she's a lovely girl," Marianne says with warm approval."

"I came to say thank you," I tell her. "Do you want to walk with me to the kennels?"

"Love to."

The path to the kennels is slightly overgrown, and along the way, I'm greeted by a few familiar faces.

"You're missed here," she tells me.

I nod. I miss the army. Adapting to civilian life often feels like I'm walking around naked—exposed, vulnerable, and unprepared for an onslaught. I'm told that feeling this way is normal. Talk therapy helps. But the future is uncertain.

"Do you know if you'll be coming back at all?"

"I've given notice," I tell her. "They are counting my sick leave as part of the twelve months. My progress is being reviewed every six weeks. If...when I'm fit for active duty again, I'll come back to work the rest."

"So your mind is made up? You're leaving for good?"

"The army has cost me too much," I confess.

"I get it. Ah, there she is!" And she points to the last kennel in a row of about forty. Fosters is lying down with her head sticking out.

"Don't look so nervous," Wilson assures me. "She'll remember you."

She doesn't come out right away. And my heart

breaks a little when I see eyes so sad. Her front leg has been amputated high up at the joint, at her chest, and she's still bandaged and wearing a cone to prevent her from tearing it. I go sit on my haunches a little way from her and call her name. Her ears twitch and she lifts her head.

"Hiya, girl. Do you remember me?"

For a long moment, she doesn't look like she's going to move, and my heart plummets. But then she gets up cautiously and hobbles up to me and nuzzles my outstretched hand.

I pat her and when I look up at Wilson, she has a hand in front of her mouth, and it looks as if she wants to cry.

"She remembers me...she actually remembers me."

Fosters and I stare into each other's eyes. Her amber eyes seem to look straight into my soul. We connect in a place where words are redundant and there's zero judgement. She needs time to heal, and so do I.

"Come, darlin', Daddy's taking you home."

Evie

ADAM TEXTS ME.

Good morning:-) how are you feeling today? Now that the tiles for the backsplash are dry and the weather being shyte, I thought I'd paint the kitchen today. Guess what colour? TEAL! I think you'd like it. Take care of yourself.x

Later.

I won the bid! One antique-claw bathtub will be delivered in the next seven days!

And then.

I hope you are okay. I think of you all day. Therapy was hard today, but at least the meds are helping me sleep. Are you getting any rest? Have you started painting again? I'm getting my thirty-day chip tomorrow. I'd really like to see you.

I text back and tell him I'd like to see the cottage. And him.

Yes! Of course, tomorrow is perfect. What time? Are you okay to drive?

You've made me the happiest man in England today. Thank you. See you tomorrow. x

I WAKE up the next day with a text from Adam waiting for me. He asks how I am, and how I'm feeling, carefully tiptoeing around and never taking the liberty to mention the baby outright. Most days I don't reply. I guess that's my way of guarding my heart. It's a feeble wall and Adam has already persistently, but with a gentle hand, engineered himself a gate. Now he stands there, asking to enter, waiting to be let in.

I try to picture Adam in therapy. It's a bittersweet pill to swallow. All I ever wanted was for him to work through his issues, but now that he's opening himself up to someone else...I feel like I don't know what my place in his life is anymore. He's given up his uniform, a job he loved, to be the man I asked him to be, and now that he has done just that—I don't know how that makes me feel.

And the fact that he isn't in uniform anymore must be hard on him. He never says he misses his job, but he must. It's like we're skating across a beautiful frozen-over pond, moving cautiously forward, foregoing the upright spins so as not to crack the thin veneer of ice before we get to the other side. We don't know how deep it is below the surface; all we know is, falling in will destroy us.

He updates me daily on the restoration of the cottage. I smiled when he told me that he's painted the walls in the kitchen teal and that he's built a stone fireplace from river rocks he collected from the stream behind the house. His next project will be the bathroom with the claw foot bath. And now I have agreed to go see him. And I do want to see him. I need to see him because I have to tell him about the job in Belgium. It all happened so fast. They offered me the job in the interview and I accepted it there and then. Time away is what I need. And while I don't expect him to really understand it, I hope he'll accept it.

I'm only just starting to show and have started looping a hair elastic around the button of my jeans, slipping it through the buttonhole in order to accommodate the swell of my lower belly. I tug at my jumper, making sure it covers my makeshift belly accommodator. I check myself in the mirror. I like myself with the bump, as tiny as it is at the moment. I smile at the thought of a bean-sized baby floating in my womb, attached by a cord like an astronaut in outer space.

I only tell Mum about my visit to Adam. Dad is still avoiding me, even though I've been home for a month already. Mum assures me that it's not shame that keeps him at a distance, but the fact that he's still processing my 'condition', coming to terms with being a grandpa. Mum gives me a batch of her homemade lavender-infused shortbread to take to Adam. I've also gotten him a gift, which feels stupid now that I'm pulling up in the driveway.

He approaches the car before I park. We smile at each other through the car window. His hands are shoved deep into his front pockets, but his eyes stay locked on mine. Alongside him is a dog, and at first, I don't see that it's missing a leg, as it cowers slightly behind Adam. When I open my car door, she overtakes Adam and rushes in to greet me with her snout.

"She won't bite. Evie, this is Fosters," Adam assures me.

I ruffle the thick pelt around her neck and roughly scratch her behind her ears, and she happily leans in for more.

"Hello, Fosters. What happened to your leg, precious?" I hear my voice take on the tone most people use when they ogle newborn babies in onesies, but one I've only ever used on dogs and cats...and bunnies. Basically anything cute and fluffy.

"She was with us on the mission when Pete died. Got wounded shortly afterwards. They asked if I wanted her and..."

"You couldn't say no."

Adam nods. "You look good," he tells me. His eyes have softened and I notice his shoulders are relaxed too. It's the physical composition of being content.

"You wouldn't say that if you saw how I had to fasten these jeans."

"Well, come on in then, let me show you around." He whistles and Fosters trots beside him.

We take our time walking the perimeter of the plot. It's not a big piece of land, but it does flank the woods and the river which gives the whole property the feeling of being endless, and the ancient trees add an element of enchantment. It's everything I loved about it when we were kids.

Inside, much still needs to be done. For the most part, it's a naked house with bare walls and floors. But he has a leather sofa and a red Persian rug in front of the massive stone hearth that stretches almost the entire length of the wall. And above the work of art, that's Adam's river-stone fireplace, hangs my painting—the one I did of this cottage for the gallery. He bought it on the night that we fought so hard, I was sure we were over forever. The night we conceived the life growing inside me.

"You bought my painting..."

"I did. I knew where it had to live. Also, I'm a huge fan of the artist."

I nod. Absorbing this information.

I turn to him. "Adam, your home is beautiful. Truly. It's everything we ever dreamed up together and more."

"Please don't say that. Don't say *your* home like you don't belong here."

Now is the time to tell him that I'm leaving England for a job in a gallery in Belgium. But I don't. Not yet. I want to skate across the ice a little longer.

"But it is your home," I say softly, "and you should be

bloody proud of it." I step closer to him and wrap my arms around him in a hug, and he responds by holding me in return. We loosen our embrace when Fosters nuzzles our knees and comes between us.

"Tea?"

"Ah, yes, that reminds me, I have something for you! Can't believe I forgot it in the car. Give me a minute."

When I come back with a biscuit tin from Mum and the tea towels I bought to match the teal wall in the kitchen, I also hand him a gift bag.

"For you."

"Evie, seriously, you didn't have to."

"I know. I wanted to. Open it!"

He pulls the tissue paper from the bag and then reveals the object wrapped in bubble wrap.

It's a teapot, the ceramic brand he's always admired in shop windows. I bought it in fire-engine red and I hoped it would remind him in some small way of happier days. His eyes light up.

"I have a feeling that I'm about to make the best cup of tea of my life."

We laugh.

I sit at the small, wooden table and watch him prepare the tea. For a moment it's hard to believe that we're estranged lovers. The familiarity that comes with knowing each other all our lives clicks us back into place like a jigsaw without us even trying. But in this moment I feel like an outsider looking in, and I like the life Adam is curating for himself.

"I need to pee," I announce as he pours the boiling water into the pot.

"Is everything alright?" His face is overcome with concern.

"Yeah, yeah, I'm fine. Just, you know, baby on bladder. Need to pee."

"Have you felt her move yet?"

I smile at the *her* but don't correct him because I think it will be a girl, too. I shake my head.

"No, but if the books are anything to go by I should be able to feel some movement pretty soon."

He nods.

"Did you know that the baby is the size of an—" I start.

"An apple," he says, finishing my sentence.

"How did you know?"

"I've been reading up online." He grins.

"Ah."

I smile to myself as I find my way to the lavatory.

When I come back down, the tea is ready and Mum's cake has found its way onto a plate in the middle of the table.

"I see your claw-foot tub has arrived. It's gorgeous."

Adam winces at my *your* again, but he manages to move past it. "It arrived this morning actually. Now all I need to do is find a plumber."

I dunk a biscuit in my tea and let it soak until just before breaking point.

Adam shakes his head and gives me a lopsided smile. "I wish you wouldn't dunk your biscuits into the tea. It ruins the tea!"

"But it enhances the flavour of the biscuit."

"Heathen," he mocks.

Our laughter evaporates in the stillness of the house.

"Evie"—Adam clears his throat from the sudden onset of hoarseness—"I wanted to ask you if I could be a part of the baby's life...a part of your life. I know I've messed up, but I'm working on my issues. I'm figuring out my next step. Please."

While he manages to keep his voice calm and measured, his eyes plead.

I reach across the table and place my hand over his.

"Adam. There's something I came to tell you. I've taken a job in Bruges at a gallery. Just temporary. Maternity cover for four months. Apparently, the person who was working the maternity cover for the manager, now needs maternity leave herself... I'm planning to be back in time for the birth." Instinctively, my hand moves from his and rests on my belly.

"You're leaving?"

"Like I said, it's just for a few months."

"Almost your entire pregnancy."

It's a statement of fact, one I've considered over and over again, always concluding that a bit of distance from everyone will do me good.

"I need this, Adam. You have your therapy and the cottage to get your head straight. I need something too. I need this time and space to make this transition." I don't tell him that I'm preparing myself for the worst—the possibility of being a single parent.

"But you could stay here. With me. Fucking hell, Evie, even staying with your parents or Gerald is better than going into hiding in Bruges!"

I take a deep breath to steady the collision of emotions coming to the fore.

"Here's the truth, Adam. I woke up one day, from my new life in London, as an up-and-coming artist, to find out I'm pregnant and my ex is the father. It's a lot to take in. I need time alone. I need to figure out who I am now. I don't know how to be a mother! I'm petrified that I'm going to really mess this up and that I might end up doing this alone!" The shrill of my panic takes up all the space in the kitchen.

Adam reaches over and cups my face. It stills me.

"You're going to be an extraordinary mother," his gentle words affirm me. His thumb wipes away a tear rolling down my cheek.

"I'm here. You're not alone. I'm not leaving you again."

I believe him. And I allow him to fold me into his arms.

"I'm scared, Adam."

"Me too."

I rest my cheek on his chest and hear the steady thump-thump of his heart.

"I'm not going to change my mind about Bruges," I whisper with all the courage I can muster, even though I'm second-guessing myself.

"I know. But we're going to work it out. Okay?"

"Okay."

THIRTEEN

ADAM

"STAY THE NIGHT," I say. More than anything, I just want Evie to be here with me.

To my surprise, she doesn't seem to hesitate. "I'd like that."

All at once, I'm aware of how unprepared I am. I worry that the house isn't warm enough, that I don't have enough bog roll or food.

"Do you want to stay with Fosters while I run down to the store?" And I hope she doesn't catch on that I'd prefer to go to the Co-op alone for a multitude of reasons. But I'm not a lucky man and I have to feign nonchalance when she replies.

"Nah, I'll come with you."

Evie insists the exercise will do her good, and so we meander down to the Co-op. We fill a basket with the ingredients for a Thai curry and ice cream for dessert;

eggs and orange juice for breakfast; and two-ply loo roll, instead of my standard cheapest on the shelf.

I leave Evie to find some popcorn while I head to the till with the basket. If a heart could turn to lead and drop into a man's shoes—that's how I felt when I saw Penny The Cashier applying her candy-floss lip gloss behind the counter. She just about snarls when she sees me. My chin drops to my chest. *Fuck my life.* Today, of all days. I look over my shoulder to find Evie beaming, shaking a packet of popcorn like she's won the golden ticket in Willy Wonka's Chocolate Factory.

I want to drop the shopping basket like it's a hot potato, but instead, I step forward and smile.

"Hey," I say, dipping my toe into the imaginary lava pool between Penny and me.

She rolls her eyes at me and starts ringing up the items one by one.

Evie sidles over brightly and drops the popcorn into the basket.

"For later," she says unnecessarily.

Penny The Cashier's eyes dart from Evie to me and back again. Then they narrow into slits, making her eyes look like the smiley eyes in Japanese cartoons because of the voluminous fake lashes.

"No Jack 'n Coke today, Adam?" She holds onto the M in my name for too long and my skin crawls.

"Not today, Penny. I quit drinking actually."

"Didya now?"

"I did."

I don't dare make eye contact with Evie, but I feel her

shoulder stiffen against mine. "Do you two know each other?"

"Oh yeah." Penny gives Evie the 'I know-know him' look before I can interject.

Evie bursts out laughing. "No, seriously, Adam?"

"What you laughing at?"

"Nothing. I just can't picture it. You're...just not his type."

"Who are you? His wife or something?"

"Something," Evie states with a flat smile.

"Thirty-seven twenty," Penny says, and she and Evie are locked in a staring contest.

I try and pull my card out as fast as I can, but Penny is in no hurry.

"Rewards card?" She's speaking to me, but she and Evie are still in check on their invisible chessboard.

"No, for fuck's sake, you know I don't have a rewards card."

"I have to ask—it's policy. Ask Raymond over there. He's the manager and my boyfriend."

I glance over and see a tall Indian boy who looks like he's nearly ready to start shaving. The poor lad is as uncomfortable as I am, shifting from one leg to the other.

I tap the card.

"There's a thirty-quid limit on the tap an' pay. Insert your card."

I want this moment to end. When I finally manage to pay, I grab the shopping bag and head for the door. I stop. Evie is leaning over the counter and in a stage whisper she asks Penny, "Was he any good?"

Penny, who has proven to be a delight, doesn't reply

but shoots her forefinger into the air, pointing to the ceiling, and then, making a sad face, curls the finger down into a sad, dysfunctional penis.

I think Evie may wet her pants she's laughing so hard while we walk home.

"Oh my God, that, what just happened in there, has just made my year! Could you really not get it up?"

I shake my head. My teeth are clenched so tight, I can't speak.

"It was a fucking disaster. I tried to get hold of you—phoned your parent's house. Your dad told me you'd moved in with your 'new fella', Gerald. I didn't go buy a bottle of Jack to look for a hook-up...but when I saw Penny...well..."

"You don't have to explain it to me. I get it. I'm not Rachel from Friends. I know we were definitely on a break."

I stop and shift the grocery bag to my other hand and take hold of Evie's wrist.

"No, Evie. You don't get it. It doesn't matter if we were on a break. I literally couldn't be with anyone else. It's like you rewired me and you're the only one..."

When we were kids, Evie would look at me like she does in this moment. Like she can see right through me—past all the bullshit. She sees me and loves me anyway. And that's why no one else will ever be able to touch my soul like she does.

"I've never been with anyone else but you," she reminds me, "and for better or worse, I've never wanted to be with anyone else."

Maybe that's why we keep orbiting each other like we

do, unable to truly pull away from each other—the fact that we were each other's first and onlys. We just fit.

When we get back to the cottage we cook together and eat at the wooden table. Afterwards, we snuggle on the sofa and watch the flames dance in the fireplace, and listen to an episode of the radio drama based on the book *The Hitchhiker's Guide to the Galaxy*.

"You do know there are audiobooks now, right?" Evie teases.

"Yeah, I know. But it gets lonely here, and let's face it, they never shut up on BBC4, do they?"

"So no TV?"

"For now? No. I'm actually thinking of getting an old-school record player."

"Vinyls! Yes!" Evie sits up. "Let's do it. Tomorrow."

I smile and agree.

Later I take Evie upstairs and we walk past three closed doors before we get to the master bedroom. I only recently bought a bed. An old, mahogany four-poster I nabbed at an open-house auction. Besides that and a chest of drawers to match, the room is completely empty.

"It echoes in here," Evie says as she surveys the magnitude of the bed, and then she turns to me. "Are all the closed doors more bedrooms?"

I nod. "They don't even have flooring yet, but I'll get there." We both look down at her belly, but before I can assure her that I can have as many rooms as she needs ready in time, she sits on the bed and swings her legs.

"You sure you're going to be okay on the sofa?"

I clear my throat a tad too loudly. Just the thought of

sharing a bed with her ignites all the desire that's been dead in me for months.

"I'll be fine."

"That's a shame. This bed"—she smooths her hands over the white linen like a seductress—"is definitely not made for one."

All I want in that moment is her hands all over me.

"You're not making this easy." The poor acoustics of the room swallows my feeble attempt at resistance.

"What's the worst that can happen?" she jokes.

I try hard to remember all the talk therapy. All things I agreed would be bad for my recovery right now. Number one: a love relationship.

"You know that more than anything I want you," I tell her, "but there's so much we need to get through. We can't keep doing this." My hands fly to the air. "We fall back on sex time and again and never resolve the important things, and it always drives us further apart. I just...I just want to do it right this time."

Her eyes are wide and I can see that my earnestness has caught her off guard. So I go, kneel in front of her, kiss her hands, and lay my head in her lap.

She strokes my hair. "I want to do things right, too."

I nod. And for the longest time, we just hold on, too afraid to be who we are without each other.

After I kiss Evie goodnight—on the forehead—and make sure she's tucked in, I add a few more logs to the fire and pull the knitted blanket under my chin. Fosters curls up on the rug, and I reach down and pat her head before I close my eyes and drift to sleep.

"Adam." Evie's voice is soft and distant, but getting louder.

I wake when she gives me a gentle shake. "Make room," she instructs as she lifts the blanket, letting the cold air in. But I comply, and shift as far back as I can to accommodate her in front of me. She tugs at a corner of the cover to cocoon herself, and it takes a bit of back and forth tugging, and half-hearted grumbling, before we settle like spoons.

"This is ridiculous. There's a massive empty bed upstairs," I mutter.

"But I couldn't sleep."

"And this is better?"

"Much." I can't see her face but I can hear her smile.

I hold her around the waist, but she guides my hand to the bump below her navel.

"She's in there," she whispers.

I picture a minute, alien-like human curled up, and snugly cradled in Evie's womb. Just a few layers of tissue, skin, and T-shirt separates my hand and the tiny person who is half me, half Evie.

I lift the old Guns 'n Roses shirt of mine Evie chose to sleep in and caress the spot I imagine the baby lies.

"Hello, Bean," I say.

Evie laughs. "Foetuses do look a bit like alien kidney beans, don't they?"

"They do."

"I like it: Bean. It has a ring to it."

The strokes on her belly become longer, my hands travelling farther afield across her body out of habit and hunger. All the way up, my fingers find her breasts fuller.

All the way down, I strum her clit, thrilled to find her pantyless.

She moans softly, and without urgency, she arches her hips for more. My cock is already rock hard, nuzzling its hungry head against her bum.

I stop. We. Should. Not. Be. Doing. This.

Evie grabs my hand and rubs herself against my palm. I've always loved how she knows her own pleasure and isn't afraid to ask for what she wants. It turns me on every time and tonight is no different.

My lips find her neck by their own volition. God, I've missed the taste and smell of this woman.

Her backside rocks against my dick, aggravating the restraint of the cotton boxers. I try to ignore my own pressing need and focus on giving her the attention she wants.

She rolls onto her back, pressing me even farther into the back cushions of the sofa, asking for more, and I comply.

She shudders, and in the dim light of the embers in the hearth, I see how her climax ripples through her whole body until she's breathless. She kisses me then, deep and slow.

"Thank you," she says, our lips almost still touching.

When she reaches for me, I stop her.

"You were perfect," I say.

She tries to protest, but I shhh her by pressing my lips against hers and kissing her with all the passion I didn't release inside her.

Afterwards, I draw her closer to me. Her head fits in my arm like it's meant to be there.

"I love you," she mutters, her words heavy with sleep.

"I love you. I'm here for you, Evie, whatever you need."

"Promise?"

I hold her tighter. Everything I've ever wanted, that's ever mattered, is right here in this room. On this sofa. In my arms.

"ADAM! ADAM! STOP!"

I'm no longer on the sofa; I'm standing over Evie who's pushing me away. My body is hot and I'm soaked with sweat. Fosters is barking, growling at me, creating a barrier between Evie and me. I look down and see my fists clenched, knuckles white.

"It was just a dream, Adam. You're okay."

I'm unprepared for what I see when I come to. Evie is sitting on the sofa, so tightly wound in terror that she looks like she wants to bolt. And the thing, the person she wants to get away from, is me.

Evie

MY JAW ACHES where Adam punched me.

One minute we were asleep on the sofa, and in the next, he was shouting something unintelligible. When I tried to wake him, he took a swing at me and connected his fist to my face with enough force that I ended up on the floor with a hard thud. Then he was up and on his feet, crying, shouting.

When Adam first got deployed, the worst of the repercussions was him having to quit the cigarettes and me pretending that I never noticed that he smelled like an ashtray. But as the years wore on and missions got longer, there would be weeks of decompression at home that involved insomnia and too much beer. He never wanted to talk about it, and he always seemed to get over it, and we carried on like normal. But this last tour, with Pete dying, and the drinking escalating...I should have known he was not okay—despite his upbeat chatter via text and all the work he's done on the cottage.

"It was just a dream, Adam. You're okay," I try to assure him.

It's scary to watch someone wake from a night terror. I saw how the veil of sleep lifted and he became conscious of the real world. And me.

"Jesus!" He comes towards me and instinctively I pull away.

"Did I—did I do that to you?"

My strong, brave Adam has crumpled to his knees, covering his face with his hands.

Fosters, sensing the danger is over, immediately walks up to her owner and licks his hands.

Adam is sobbing. I sit beside him and put an arm around his shoulder.

"I know you didn't mean to. You were having a dream. I'm okay."

But he shakes his head. "I hit you."

"You didn't know what you were doing."

A heavy, sad silence brews in the room.

"You should go," he tells me, turning his face away, eyes intent on something in the distance.

I stand up. "I'm not going anywhere, Adam Taylor. I'm not leaving so that you can beat yourself up and do something stupid."

"I'm trying to protect you...and the baby." His voice cracks at the last part.

"Look at me. Look at me, Adam."

He winces when he turns to me, and I imagine my jaw is already starting to swell and bruise.

"I am not made of glass. I won't just break. I am okay...or I will be when I get some ice on this whopper."

Making light of the incident doesn't even elicit a smile from Adam. But he does get up, and I follow him to the fridge.

He hands me a bag of frozen peas wrapped in a dish towel.

"I don't have any ice."

I press the cool bag against the hit and flinch at the pressure on the tender tissue. I manage a smile, recalling the time I iced his hand with a bag of frozen Brussels sprouts.

"Can you take any painkillers?" He looks at my stomach instead of me.

"I'm okay. It's not that bad. Won't say no to a cup of tea though."

He doesn't move, but I know that twitch in his jaw. He's getting angry and trying to control it.

"Hey, do you remember that time I iced your hand with a bag of frozen Brussel sprouts? After you punched

Jimmy..." My attempt to make light of the situation is failing miserably.

"Why are you still here? If you know what's good for you and the...you should go. I'm no good to you, Evie. Your father was right about me, I'm bad news. Damaged goods."

I shake my head. This cottage-restoring Adam reminds me of the Adam I fell in love with. He is open and vulnerable again. Yesterday, I saw a version of him I hadn't seen in years: a man getting comfortable in his own skin, facing his demons without the self-destructive crutch of booze. I don't think he's aware that the irony of his transformation into the man I need is the guy he was when we met. He hasn't changed; he's just become more of himself.

"I refuse to believe it. Adam, you've got issues—we all do. But you're working on them. That's what matters to me. I've known you all my adult life, and I know you would never, ever lift a hand to me. I know that, and so,do you."

"But I hit you, Evie. There's the proof." He points at the homemade compress I'm still using to soothe my jaw.

"You didn't know what you were doing."

"Exactly! That makes me dangerous."

"You'll get through this, Adam. You have to. Do you want to be a part of Bean's life?"

He nods.

"Then start by making us a cup of tea. I believe we have a record player to buy?"

"Evie—"

"No. We're done talking about it now."

"Okay, but I have a meeting today."

"Oh."

"Do you want to come? I'm getting my thirty-day chip."

I give Adam a small, painful smile. "It's a date!"

FOURTEEN

ADAM

DESPITE MY PROTESTATIONS, Evie and I get ready to go to my meeting and then shopping for the record player.

When she steps out of the shower, I see her fully naked for the first time in months. Her lithe, girl-like body has altered. Her hips are softer, her nipples darker, and her skin glows like somebody has lit a torch inside her, making her luminosity mesmerising. She flashes me a smile and then instantly grimaces. Her jaw is a messy blend of dark blue and red.

It kills me to see her like that. Marred. Hurt by me. Never in my life has the thirst for a drink been this bad. It's good that she's spending the day with me; otherwise, my thirty-day chip would be nothing to celebrate at all.

"I'll need to go to Mum's and pick up more clothes."

"I don't think your father will want to see me."

"Don't mind Daddy. He will get over himself; he always does."

EVERYONE TURNS to look at us when we enter the church hall where the AA meeting is held.

"You must be Evie," Danny says, extending a hand.

"This is Danny, my sponsor," I introduce them.

"There's tea and coffee on the table. Please, help yourself."

Evie nods and smiles. She's done a good job covering the bruise on her face with make-up and wearing a scarf wrapped all the way up to her chin.

"Are you sure you want to be here?" I ask. When I look around the room I suddenly see everything through Evie's eyes. Some of the people here are at their rock bottom. Self-care is out of the window. Their clothes have old stains on them and bear witness to binges. Men are unshaved and the women have long, unkempt hair. They've lost everyone and everything that matters to them. Some are drunk right now, and have only come because of the free coffee and biscuits, having nowhere else to go.

"Adam..."

"I know. Some of the guys are really on the down and out."

"Can we do something to help them?"

I shake my head. "That's not how it works. They have to help themselves. Being here is helping them."

We sit in the circle, and everyone introduces them-selves as addicts. A few share the highs and lows of the past week. When it comes to my turn, I decide to share even though it feels like unzipping my skin, raw and painful.

"This is my partner, Evie." Everyone says hi to Evie. Jo, one of the women, gives her a little wave.

"She came over to see me yesterday for the first time since I quit drinking...that was my twenty-ninth day sober. And I felt amazing. And then..."

Evie squirms in the chair next to mine and gives me a *you don't have to tell them* look.

"And everything was going well...until last night."

Somebody lets out a cat-call whistle and there are a lot of woohoos, and someone even claps. It makes everyone laugh.

"No...no that's not what I want to talk about."

The token boos die down.

"I must have been having a dream, I don't remember. But when I came to, I saw that I had hit Evie." I wipe a stray tear off my cheek and clear my throat.

"Evie, being who she is, forgave me the moment it happened, but every time I see the bruise on her face, I hate myself. I wanted her to leave so that I could find a bottle, you know? But she stayed. She helped me stay sober another day."

Everyone claps. When I look at Evie, she's crying and she reaches over and hugs me.

"I'm so proud of you," she whispers.

Danny stands up and calls me over. I receive my thirty-day token. And of all the achievements of my life, this is the most significant.

. . .

WE ARE both quiet in the car as I drive us to her parents' house. It's been a long time since the silence between us has been this content. Tender. For so long I believed that I wasn't allowed to show weakness, that Evie and the world required me to be impenetrable to all the hardships life has thrown my way. I've lived for so long, shaking off disappointments, anger, and pain—'manning up' and 'moving along'—that this feeling of utter emotional nakedness is as much foreign as it's terrifying. I sneak a glance at Evie in the passenger seat, worried that I've let her see too much of the ugly in me, but when she catches my eye, she smiles and stretches her hand out to squeeze my thigh. Then she leaves her hand there, and I cover it with my own. This moment, this feeling, is how it used to be when we first fell in love...before I started competing with her father for all he gave her. I was a fool.

Before long we are pulling up in the driveway of her parents' home—a wide, pebbled lane, that circles an island of perfectly manicured lawn, with an antique sundial at its centre.

Evie must sense my trepidation, as she gives my thigh a reassuring squeeze before I hurry out of the car to open her door for her.

To my surprise, Mr Simpson receives me with a cool handshake but with a commendable effort to draw me back into the family. This gnaws at my guilt about the repercussions of my night terror, but we all play our part in keeping the peace for Evie's sake.

Her mom hugs me tightly and behaves like she just saw me last week.

"Evie tells us you're renovating the cottage outside of the village?"

"I am. Still lots to do."

"Mum, you should see what Adam has done with the place. He has a six-foot fireplace built from river stones. And the bath…"

"…Which I still need to install," I remind her.

"The bath is a claw-foot. Just stunning."

Evie's dad nods in the direction of the patio door, and this is my invitation to join him for a man-to-man, but mainly because he wants to light up a cigar. He hands me a whiskey in a cut-crystal tumbler.

"No thanks," I say. And his gaze flits from me to Evie. Then he shrugs and adds the rich, amber liquid to his own glass. I follow him outside and take a seat opposite him.

"So you bought the house?"

"Cash. It wasn't expensive. It needed a lot of work. A new roof, for one."

He nods. "And the renovations? Got a loan?"

"Not that it's any of your business, with all due respect, but no. I'm using my savings."

He considers me, and it reminds me of how a snake surveys its prey on those nature programmess on TV.

"It's all good news, Adam. With the little one on the way, we only want what's best for Eve and the baby. We want to be assured that they are provided for."

Why does it feel like I'm interviewing for a job that's rightfully mine? "I will provide for my family. That's not even a question."

But he dismisses my assurance. "There's something

else." He takes a long puff of his cigar and squints as the smoke assaults his face. "After we found out about Evie's condition...well, it got me thinking about genetics and how little we know about your side of the family."

My head hangs of its own accord. "I'm an orphan," I say out loud. "I know no more than you do about my bloodline, Mr Simpson. Surely you can't hold that against me? It's out of my control."

I can feel the heat rise in my neck.

He raises a hand to still my impending explosion. "I know that's not your fault, son. That's not where I'm going. But...haven't you always wondered where you came from? Who your birth mother is?"

An adopted kid spends most of his childhood hung on searching the face of every woman he meets, desperate to find some resemblance. But I don't tell Richard Simpson that. I don't tell him that I stopped looking after Evie came into my life and filled all the voids I hid away from the world with love. I don't say anything. I just shake my head as if it has never crossed my mind.

"Well, I thought so much. So I took the liberty to hire a private investigator."

I blink. "What?"

"I found your birth mother. She lives in Sheffield."

I'm still sitting, dumbstruck, when Evie joins us.

"Adam?" She's put a hand on my shoulder, but I don't have words to speak.

"Daddy? What's going on?"

Her father leans forward in his seat and tips the ash

off the end of the thickly rolled Cuban. He clears his throat.

"I was just telling Adam that I tracked down his birth mother. She's in Sheffield."

"Daddy! You're un-fucking-believable!" Evie is just about growling at her father while her mother does her best to blend into the background.

"How dare you," she says, and then she spits at her mother, as well. "And you! To have the audacity to get involved in Adam's personal life! If he wanted to find his mother, he would have by now! How dare you!"

"Eve, calm down," her mother chides. "It's not good for you to get all worked up like this."

"You should have thought of that before you started meddling in something that has nothing to do with you!"

I sit with my head in my hands, trying to process the information.

"I was only trying to help!" Mr Simpson tries to defend himself, but Evie isn't done with him yet.

"You're always trying to fix everything and then you make it worse! Stop ruining people's lives!"

"Stop." I stand up and sidle up to Evie. "Your mom is right—you need to take a deep breath and just calm down, okay?"

She glares at me, but I ignore it. I turn to Mr Simpson.

"What you did was...definitely overstepping. And a year ago I would have told you to go fuck yourself." Now it's my turn to raise my hand and veto his interruption. I look at Evie and then at my unofficial in-laws, the only constant parental role models I've had in my life since I was seventeen. "But I think you're right. If you know who she is and where she is, and if she wants to meet me, then I'd very much like to meet the woman who gave me up."

A satisfied smile of vindication spreads over Mr Simpson's mouth for a moment before he sucks on his cigar again.

"Really?" Evie asks me in earnest. "You don't have to go through with it just to please him."

"I know, darling. It's not that. In my mind, she's some junkie who got knocked up, and found out too late and had to give me up. If that's true, I'm finally ready to face it. I have to face it."

Mr Simpson nods his head in agreement. "Good on you, my boy."

———

LATER THAT NIGHT Evie and I lie in the four-poster at the cottage, listening to Guns 'n Roses on vinyl. The cry in Axl Rose's voice in "November Rain" gives me goosebumps every time.

"You surprised me today," she says, drawing nondescript patterns on my chest with her forefinger. "I didn't know you wanted to find your mother."

I sigh. "As crazy as it is, your dad has always been so hard on me, but I still look up to him. He's a man that has it all and has it all together, you know what I mean? I guess, what I'm saying is that I care what he thinks. And maybe he has a point—I'm going to be a dad myself in a couple of months. I need to know where I come from."

"You're the bravest person I know," she tells me.

"No varnish can hide the grain of the wood; and that the more varnish you put on, the more the grain will express itself." I quote her a line from my favourite book.

If there was ever a time for me to strip off the varnish and get back to the grain of myself, the time is now.

FIFTEEN

Evie

ADAM IS DRIVING me to Bruges. I traded my Mini Cooper for something that can better accommodate a car seat in the future, and Adam helped me choose the mini SUV. It's packed to the brim.

"Do you think Fosters will be okay with my parents?"

"I think she will get spoiled rotten." He turns to me. "Don't worry, I'll bring her when I come to visit in a couple of weeks."

"That will be good. Thank you for driving me." I rest my hand on his thigh, and he covers it with his own.

It's a six-hour trek across the country. The first four and a half gets us to Dover, where we take the channel tunnel to Calais. Once we've parked the car in the train, Adam gets out to stretch his legs, and I do the same, except I also hunt for a loo.

I wonder now if I've made the right choice to take the

job in Bruges. A few weeks ago, Bruges seemed like the perfect city to find myself again—as an artist and a mother. Now I wonder how I will get through the weeks without Adam's affection. But we don't talk about that. Instead, we spend most of the journey in companionable silence, listening to an audiobook.

"Are you hungry?"Adam tries to hand me one of Mum's egg-mayo sandwiches. I wave the oozy triangle away.

"Banana?"

"Stop trying to feed me, I'm fine!"

"Alright, alright." He pulls me into his arms and holds me.

"I just worry about you," he whispers.

I nod my head against his chest, but my doubts are gnawing harder and more insistently the closer we get to Bruges.

The automated intercom announcement in the train gives us the warning that we are minutes away from disembarking, and we get back into the car.

"Last leg." Adam smiles. But all I can do is nod.

Less than an hour later, we arrive at my new abode. Since we crossed the channel, Adam and I haven't really spoken. It's like this with us. When our emotions are high, we often can't talk about them, but I feel it. I feel his sadness expand the closer we get to Bruges; I feel it and my body responds with an empty ache. I miss him already. Despite the fact that coming to Bruges was my idea, I already know that the niggly emptiness I'm starting to feel isn't going to go away.

Adam does his best to be upbeat when the cottage comes into view.

My one-bed cottage is a converted outbuilding on a large property that was historically a farm, eventually sold off piecemeal as the need for residential property grew. But the main farmhouse remained, with a couple of its outbuildings. The current owners rent out the cottages as secondary income streams to support their craft-beer business.

They introduce themselves as the Queens of the Castle, and at once start flirting with my fit, dark-haired, blue-eyed boy. Adam takes it in his stride.

Later, when the last of the suitcases and boxes are in the cottage, Adam helps me make up the bed.

"The Queens like you," I tease.

"Stop it. I was just being friendly. Wait, you're not jealous, are you?"

"No. I know you're mine," I tell him matter-of-factly, with a twinge of jealousy which I try to hide.

"I am," he responds without a moment's hesitation.

The truth is, ever since I went to visit Adam at the cottage, when I saw how hard he had worked on building, literally building us a home, my heart started to heal. I started to see a future for us, and our family.

I crawl across the freshly made bed until I'm on my knees in front of Adam. I unbuckle his belt, pull open his button fly in one smooth motion.

"Oh God, Evie." Adam tilts my head up and lowers his head to kiss me, and I feel the pressure between my legs and the slow warmth of desire spread throughout my body.

I reach for him, but he stops me.

"I can't, Evie. God, I want you. But I made myself a promise. One hundred days of sobriety before I give in to my other addiction...you."

My eyes go wide. "But you just got your thirty-day chip..."

"Eight days ago. Yes, I'm painfully aware." His eyes briefly flit to the bulge in his boxers.

I pull away.

"Hey," he says, taking hold of my arm, "where do you think you're going?"

"But you said—"

"My self-deprivation is a much-needed exercise of restraint, but that doesn't mean I have any intention of not meeting your needs."

"I'm happy to hear that," I say, doing my best to be coy, "because I've heard that orgasms are like hugs for the baby."

"Well, in that case..."

When he kisses me again, I let his hands roam over every inch of skin, explore every fold. When he starts using his tongue, I lie back and lose myself in delicious ecstasy.

The next day, we spend the best part of the day on foot, taking in the sights of the tiny city. We go to the *Frietmuseum,* a place dedicated to the history and making of fries. We drink hot chocolate, stirring blocks of fine milk chocolate, set on sticks, into steaming mugs of milk. We walk idly along the canals and watch the tourists snap pictures from the boats below.

"This town is kind of magical. I can see why you

want to work here," Adam tells me as we stand in the market square and squint at the high clock tower.

I agree.

ADAM

WE PLAN FOR FORTNIGHTLY VISITS, with me making the trips to Belgium to see Evie. I leave on Thursday afternoons and return to England on Monday afternoons, giving us three full days together twice a month.

The first month, everything goes smoothly, but then I get the call that I'm cleared for active duty just six weeks after the weekend that I helped Evie move.

"I can't wait to see you; I'm literally counting the hours," she says to me over the phone.

I hate to disappoint her, but we both knew there was a possibility that I would be cleared for duty and would get called back to work out my notice period.

"There's something I have to tell you, darling," I say as gently as I can muster.

"Did the tiles for the bathroom arrive?"

"Yes, but no. That's not what I meant to tell you."

"Okay..."

I take a deep breath. " Darling, I've been recalled to active duty."

Silence. And then I hear her cry.

"Oh, baby, please don't cry."

"When do you have to report back?"

"Monday."

Another painful silence.

"Are you still coming to see me?"

"Of course I am, but I'll have to leave on Sunday."

"I'm scared, Adam. I don't want you to go back to Afghanistan."

"I know. Let's just wait till Monday to hear where I'm going to be posted, okay? The army owns me for another nine months. If they want their pound of flesh, they're entitled to it."

Evie immediately starts bawling over the phone and I instantly regret the turn of phrase.

Fuck.

It takes a while, but eventually, she can talk again without crying.

"Good news though," I try to cheer her up, "I'm meeting Patty for coffee next Friday."

"So, the phone call went well?"

"Well, as good as it could have. I mean, she was way calmer than I would be if some guy called me up to say he was my son."

"How did she sound?" Evie prods in her gentle way.

"Nice, actually. Educated," I concede.

"Did she tell you if you had any siblings?"

"No," I tell her, making sense of the conversation as I talk things through with Evie, "I think she wants to check me out first. Fair enough, I want to do the same. We're meeting halfway in Birmingham."

"Wish I could be there with you." She sighs, and I can hear that her mouth is close to the receiver. It makes me miss her even more. So close yet so far.

"I wish you were here, but I think this is something I need to do alone," I tell her and she agrees with me.

After we say goodbye, I feed Fosters and put a record on the turntable. I listen to Neil Diamond and Elvis while I work on my next project, a cot for the baby.

WHEN I ENTER the coffee shop, it's not Patty I recognise, though she did tell me she'd be wearing a red jumper. The person I see first is the man sitting beside her. His raven-coloured hair is salt and pepper at the temples and his blue eyes match mine.

My head is reeling. I came here to meet my biological mother. Could this man sitting next to her be my father? It's unlikely. Perhaps he's an uncle or another relative.

"Adam?" She stands up and invites me to sit down, her brown eyes drinking me in. I can feel it, and I sit down and study her just the same. Even though there isn't much resemblance, when she smiles, I know where I got my dimple from.

It's awkward—three strangers sitting at a table, trying to establish a connection.

"Thank you for coming," I say, but I can't hide the trembling in my voice.

"We're so glad you found us." Patty flashes her dimple again, and I see her eyes are brimming with tears. She reaches across the table and squeezes my hand.

I look from Patty to the man yet to be introduced to me. But he, too, is holding back tears. His bottom lip quivers. He pulls a handkerchief from his pocket and blows his nose.

"Who is he?" I finally ask.

Patty looks at me in surprise and then turns to the man beside her before taking his hand and joining it to our hands which are still clasped together in the middle of the table.

"Adam, didn't they tell you? This is your father, Robert."

I want to say something, but I'm at a loss. Then the tea arrives and I watch Robert first pour the milk, then add the sugar and stir before he adds the tea from the pot. It's like watching an older version of myself. I listen to Patty's story, which is also my story. But not one that I know.

Patty and Robert fell in love in high school. She was just sixteen when she got pregnant. Her parents sent her off to a convent in Wales where she gave birth to me and was forced to give me up after only being allowed to see me for five minutes after the birth. Her parents made sure the adoption was closed so that she could carry on with her life. Finish school and all of that. Which she did. She even went to university and is now a primary school teacher. She and my father never stopped loving each other. He became an engineer and they got married when they were twenty. They have two more sons, my full brothers. Leo is twenty-six and Robby is twenty-one.

I take this information in slowly. Not all of it penetrates straight away. Some of it seems to slide right off me as I just can't comprehend the fact that I'm sitting here in front of both my parents. That I have a whole family, including brothers. And the struggles I went through the first sixteen years of my life could have been avoided. I had parents all along. There was no reason for me to end up moving from foster home to foster home after my adoptive parents split up and basically gave me back to the orphanage, and I became the state's problem, except that I was let down by the system. Sure, I never went hungry and always had a bed to sleep in, but I didn't know love as a child. I didn't know love or how to give love until I met Evie.

"I'm so glad they let you keep your name," Patty says.

"You named me?"

"Yes. I did."

I nod.

"I want you to know that giving you up was the hardest thing I've ever done. I've thought of you every day of my life, Adam. Your dad and I sometimes sit and wonder out loud where you are and how your life has turned out. And to see you...to see you here: handsome, polite. It makes us so proud, son. So, so proud. Here..." She draws a bundle of sealed envelopes from her handbag. All of them are addressed to me.

"I wrote to you. Mostly on your birthday, but sometimes I just wanted to speak to you..." She slides the envelopes across the table.

I jerk my hand away. I'm suffocating. It's all too much.

"Excuse me." I get up and go outside for air.

My head is spinning. My heart is racing. I don't know what to do. I thought the worst thing I could find out was that my mother was a druggie. But it turns out that the worst thing I could find out is that she isn't. That if only I'd been born to the same parents one or two years later, I could have grown up in a normal home with a normal family.

I call Evie and she picks up on the second ring.

"Adam? What's going on? Is she awful?"

"No." I barely get the word out. I'm choking on the tears I'm fighting hard to keep under control.

"No?"

"She's married to my father and I have two brothers." I blurt it all out.

"Your mother and father married each other?"

"Yes."

"But why did they give you up?" Her voice is small and sad on the other side of the line. As always, Evie shows my suppressed emotions by being open with her own.

"She was young," I explain, "seventeen. Her parents made her. She's a teacher now."

"Adam...that's amazing." Evie doesn't say it's also devastating, but I think we both feel it.

"I guess," I say under my breath.

"You're angry." She states it like it's a fact, which, in this moment it is.

I don't answer.

"I get that. But I also feel sorry for her. You're not the only victim here, Adam. You went through hell growing up, but they did, too. Imagine you have no idea where Bean is but every day you have to get up and get on with life. That could not have been easy either."

She's right.

When I take my place at the table with my parents, I tell them about foster care. Patty and Robert both hang their heads and cry. But I assure them I was okay. That my life became infinitely better when I met Evie.

"I joined the army at seventeen."

"And Evie?"

"She's an artist, working in Bruges until the baby will be born."

"You're going to be a dad?"

I nod. "Yes, and I guess that means you will be grand-parents."

We spend another hour sharing snippets of our lives with each other. The waitress reminds us that they are closing in fifteen minutes.

"Can we take you to dinner, son?" Robert asks me as we step out into the dark winter night.

"No, thank you. I have to head back. But, if it's okay with you, I'd like to meet up again sometime?"

"Can I call you?" Patty asks.

"Anytime," I tell her, and really mean it.

We say goodnight and I start to walk away, but Patty tugs at my coat and pulls me into her arms, and holds me tight.

"Please forgive me," she whispers over and over again.

"I do, Mum. I do."

SIXTEEN

Evie

I CAN'T HELP IT. I talk to the baby. I tell her all about her dad finding his parents and that she has uncles now, as well.

Even though Adam and I are long distancing, this time is good for me. Every day, I walk to work from my little cottage, and even though I'm not actively painting, I find that I'm fulfilled by the day-to-day job of managing the small gallery. I meet local artists, appraise works, and chat with customers. Turns out GCSE French is coming in handy although I'm still really rusty.

Gerald calls me often and we talk for hours. I cosy up on the sofa with a freshly made Belgian chocolate drink. He's met someone, and this has finally given him the push he's needed to come out.

"Is it appropriate to throw a coming-out party?" he asks me over the phone.

"Um, maybe. Who would you invite?"

"All my queer friends, of course." I literally hear him tut on the end of the line.

"But, Gerry, they all already know you're gay. That's not much of a coming out, is it?"

There's a moment of silence before I hear one of his dramatic sighs. "Okay. You make a valid point. You want me to invite Daddy."

I smile on the other end of the line. "Now, that will make it a real coming-out party."

"Mmmm," he says, but I can tell he isn't convinced, and as a result, he turns the conversation in my direction.

"You and Adam still good?" he asks, and I can hear he still has some reservations about Adam being back in my life.

"We're good," I reassure him, "taking it one day at a time."

"Do you know if he is being sent back to Afghan?"

I pause, taking a sip of my hot chocolate. Even though Adam has given his notice, getting pulled into active duty could mean anything from a safe office job at home or being posted off to a warzone. And then he wouldn't have a choice; he'd have to go.

"I don't know. It's possible. I mean he has given his notice; there's not much more he can do."

Long after the call with Gerald, the seed of worry that Adam could be called back into active duty starts taking root. I find myself soothing the baby growing inside me even though he or she is oblivious to the situation.

. . .

IT FEELS strange to be back in uniform. I don't recall ever feeling so restricted by the hard material and indestructible stitching. I know it must be my mental state because with all the work on the house, I've lost weight and the shirt and trousers are baggier than usual.

I report to Captain Meyer, who stands up from behind his desk and salutes me in return.

"Sit down, Staff. You did one helluva job for us in Nahar-e Saraj. We all feel the loss of Sergeant Anderson. He was one of a kind."

I nod in agreement.

"And you, you underwent some therapy, and I'm told you're mentally fit for duty again, and by the looks of it, you should have no problem passing the fitness test tomorrow morning."

"Yes, sir."

"Is there some hesitation in your voice, Staff?"

"Sir, I've already handed in my resignation. I'm hoping to work out my time on home soil, if that's possible."

Meyer studies me from behind his desk.

"That's not how the army works, Staff. But even if it did, I'm surprised. You've always excelled out in the field."

"With respect, sir, my priorities have changed."

When the captain sits back in his chair, I take it as a sign to speak freely.

"Evie is pregnant...and I bought a small house. I guess

I just want to be around as much as possible." *And not die*, but I don't say the last part out loud.

The captain nods, I see understanding in his eyes. But I know it doesn't really matter how much sympathy the man may have for my situation. In the end, if there's work to be done, I'll have to go, and not even he can save me from it.

"The good news is that for now, we need you here for training. The new recruits have chosen their areas of specialty, and your knowledge and experience will go a long way in preparing these boys for their deployment."

"Thank you, sir."

"Dickens, this doesn't mean you can't be called up. When the time comes, we'll send who we need—and that may be you."

"Yes, sir. Is there anything else?"

"Yes, actually. How's Fosters?"

I stay a little while longer and we chat about Fosters' remarkable recovery.

"I'm glad she got a home with a man of your calibre, Dickens. I wish I could change your mind about leaving the army, but I can see I'd be wasting my time. Just know, we will miss you here."

"Thank you, sir."

When I step out of his office and shut the door behind me, I pause to remember to breathe. This calms the emotions building up like a rain cloud in my chest.

Leaving the army won't be easy. It's been my constant of constants. No matter what, I always had the lads and this job that was important—saving lives. It fulfilled me…but it also broke me. It's time to move on, but that doesn't mean it won't hurt to say goodbye.

———————

I ARRIVE in Bruges two days later and drive directly to Evie's cottage where I park the car. It's an easy ten-minute walk from here to the gallery. As usual, the pedestrian sidewalks and narrow cobbled streets are busy with tourists. It's cold and getting dark fast, so I pick up my pace.

The glass door already has the CLOSED sign displayed, and I can see Evie behind the counter, writing in a large leather-bound book. I knock softly, and she looks up and smiles. God, she is exquisite. Her hair has grown over the last few months and she's kept the pregnancy glow. When she steps out from behind the counter, I can't help but smile. Her belly is now the size of a watermelon and she carries it all in front like a beachball tucked under her dress.

"Hello, darling," I say, pulling into her the moment I step into the shop.

She kisses me back, shutting the door with an arm over my shoulder and a flick of the wrist.

We kiss for a long time. It's been two weeks since we last saw each other. For a little more than two months now, we've been living this way—together, apart.

"Hey, soldier," she says when we finally pull away, "you're earlier than I expected."

"I gave some training today and the guys finished early, so I took liberty."

"Shocking!" she mocks me. And then she steps a few paces back.

"Have you seen this?" She points to her belly. "It's like it just popped out overnight!"

"Swell," I tease.

"Grrrr. It would be fine if I had clothes that fit, but right now, I'm living in tights, long shirts, and this dress."

"Are you trying to tell me we'll be spending tomorrow shopping for clothes?" I ask, trying to disguise my disappointment and reluctance.

"I'd never do that to you!" She laughs. "I have people for that."

"Oh yeah?"

"Mum and Gerry. They're coming over next week with some 'season essentials', as Gerry puts it."

"Excellent. Does that mean I can take you home and ravish you now?"

"Easy, soldier. Mamma's gotta eat."

"I like the sound of that," I say, closing in on her, grabbing her bum, and pressing her against me.

She laughs. "No, like, as in, if I don't get a plate of butter chicken and an extra-large naan right now, I'm going to start crying."

I let go of her perfect bum and drop my chin to my chest. "Alright then. C'mon, let's go. I saw a little place nearby."

I put my hand on Evie's belly and talk to Bean. "Survival tip number one kiddo: feed the mamma to avoid the hangry—trust me on this."

Evie gets her wish and we eat curry at a small restaurant on one of the side streets. It's an odd place where the owner is British but dresses in traditional Indian attire. But the peculiarity is soon swept out of our minds with the rich, mouthwatering spice aromas that waft onto our table from the kitchen.

"I've been chatting to Patty," I tell Eve while we tear and savour warm, buttery naan while we wait for the mains.

"You're still calling her Patty? Okay. What's she like?"

"Nice. Like too nice. She asked me if I wanted to play golf with Robert. Me? Golf!" I laugh at my own joke.

"Well, you should."

I glare at Evie. "What? No. I don't play golf. Ask your father, he will happily concur." I bury my head in my hands.

"Oh shut up. Daddy is too uppity. It'll be different with your own dad. Besides, golf is more about the nine-teenth hole than anything else."

"Yeah, and I don't partake."

"I know that, but you're missing the point. He wants to get to know you. You want that, right?"

I nod.

"Well, then. Go play golf."

I agree but I'm not entirely convinced I want my father to find out I'm rubbish at games. My pendulum of participation in just about anything alternates between aggressively competitive to not giving a shit—and nothing in between.

When we get back to the cottage, it seems much later than it really is. It's the end of October and already, the long, dark nights of winter are creeping up on us and robbing us of the daylight.

Evie immediately starts running herself a bath and half instructs, half invites me to join her. I don't put up a fight. I got my ninety-day chip ten days ago, so that makes today day one hundred of sobriety. My self-imposed celibacy is over and not a day too soon. If Evie had let me, I would have taken her right there and then in the shop.

Just the thought of having her bent over the pristine glass counter in the bespoke art gallery makes me lecherous. Suddenly I'm worried about being too hungry for her, about possibly hurting her.

I climb into the bath and bury myself under the foam. The hot water is already doing its job of easing the stiffness in my hamstrings from all the drills I've been doing with the squad to keep our fitness up.

"I see the bath called your name," Evie says as she walks in. Her silk nightgown is tied in a careless knot above the swell of her stomach, exposing the length of her inner thigh all the way to the top.

My cock stands at attention and I curse under my breath. As much as I want tonight to be slow so that I can savour every inch of her, I feel like a pubescent schoolboy who can't control his John Thomas.

Evie lights a few candles and switches off the light. "Much better," she says, her eyes seductively fixed on mine.

Then she loosens the poor excuse of a tie, and allows the delicate fabric to fall to the floor. I can't take my eyes off her body. The soft curvature of her hips and heavy, full breasts are a wonder.

"Some men love their women with child...others can't stand it. Which are you, Adam Taylor?" she asks, hesitating, waiting for my answer before she joins me in the suds.

I swallow hard. "Definitely the former," I assure her.

Evie

ADAM MUST BE crazy if he thinks I've forgotten about his hundredth day of sobriety. I've been dreaming day and night about tonight since day thirty-eight—and finally, here we are.

I slip into the bath with him, sitting on the opposite end of the tub. Our legs are over-under, with mine being over.

"I have something on my mind," I say to him in my best 'this is serious' tone.

He sits up a little, a cloud of worry passing over his face. It's so deeply genuine that I decide to end my feigned ignorance of his milestone.

"What is it?" he asks.

"Nothing bad...it's just that I can't stop thinking about the fact that today is your hundredth day without a drink and that means..." I let my voice trail off and slide my foot up his thigh to the junction at the very top. He shifts. And I use my toes to tease him.

"You thought I'd forgotten, didn't you?"

He nods. "I—"

"Don't speak. Just...relax."

I position myself on my knees, taking up the space between his thighs. I want to kiss him, but that always drives us too fast. Instead, I lay my hands on his hard pectorals and gently massage them, moving up to his shoulders and neck. I watch how he uncoils, slowly loosening the tightness in his shoulders. He closes his eyes and rolls his head in a half-moon from one side to the other.

I smile at his appreciative "mmmm," as I knead the tension out of them. Then I move my efforts upwards, onto his head. I press my fingers onto his scalp and start massaging in small, circular motions until I have to lean into him to reach the nape of his neck.

Adam stays still, releasing the occasional moan as the tension drains from his body.

I press hard into the soft spot at the base of his skull, knowing full well, this is the end and the beginning. When I sit back, Adam wastes no time. He takes a sponge and squeezes waterfalls over my breasts as he leans in to kiss me.

He parts my lips with restrained gentleness, and it leaves me unprepared for the insistence and urgency at which he draws me into this dance. We kiss like we always do when we're at the cusp of our sex—hard, deep. He tugs at my bottom lip, and I flinch at the delicious sting of pain which escalates the ache in me to be filled.

The bathwater has long gone cold, and without a word passing between us, we both get out. Him first, and I, after being offered his hand. We don't dry off. We don't speak. He scoops me up without the slightest effort and carries me to the bedroom.

Adam takes his time with me. Hands, lips, tongue traverse across the plains and peaks of my new shape. I lie back and lose myself in the pleasure of the sensations that seem to be awakening parts of me bit by bit: skin, heart, clit. He teases me there, flicking his tongue over the swollen bud before he covers it with the warmth of his mouth. My moaning emboldens his efforts, and within seconds, I'm begging, my body writhing under him, greedy for more, more, more.

He tests my readiness with a finger and then two. It's a cruel delaying tactic that I don't care for, and I curse him to let him know I've waited long enough.

"I don't want to hurt you," he tells me, and I can hear in his voice that exercising so much control is killing him.

"Adam"—I call his eyes to mine—"come here."

He leans in and I hook my hand behind his neck and take his lips captive. When I pull away, I tell him to fuck me.

SEVENTEEN

ADAM

"WISH ME LUCK," I say with more trepidation than enthusiasm to Evie on the other end of the line. I'm standing at the boot of the car, and across the car park, I can see Robert waiting for me at the entrance. I give him a quick wave. I always feel like a clown when I'm wearing golf clothes.

"Gerry wants to know if you're wearing any tartan." Evie is giggling and clearly enjoying Gerry's flamboyant company.

"Tell Gerry to go—"

"Bye! Love you! Remember, it's all in the wrist!"

"You're not bloody helping. Bye."

I hang up and hitch the golf bag I loaned from Evie's dad on my shoulder and slam the boot shut a bit harder than necessary, and walk to meet Robert.

"Everything alright?" Robert's intense blue eyes are

riveted to mine as I approach. They are hard to look away from, mainly because they are my eyes. They settle and unsettle me in a confusion of emotions. I manage a weak smile.

"I'm not much of a golfer...or as Evie's father has told me—I'm not a golfer's backside!"

"He sounds delightful." Robert smiles.

"You have no idea."

A hip guy in his mid-twenties makes his way to us. He not only looks the part in his tailored shorts, expensive haircut, and ridiculously white shoes, this guy has rich and groomed written all over him. He throws a hand over his shoulder and beeps his sports car to lock it. I don't know him, but he's the kind of lad I'd happily lay into at a pub after a few, wiping that idiotic smile right off his pretty, little face.

"Ah, here he is!" Robert says cheerily. "Adam, this is your brother Leo. Leo this is Adam."

Fucking hell.

"It's so nice to finally meet you, mate," Leo says with a smile that reaches all the way to the family eyes.

"Hey," I manage and am pleasantly surprised that his handshake is not at all soft and doughy.

"Robby should've been here by now," Robert says, at which Leo informs me that our baby brother has never been on time for anything in his whole life.

"The only reason he has managed to stay employed is because he works from home," Leo adds.

Robert steps away and takes out his phone to call the missing player.

"So, you guys do this often?" I ask, trying to assess how badly this situation can go for me.

"Play golf? Hell no. About twice a year, Dad gets a bee in his bonnet about 'connecting' as a family, and Rob and I agree to play for a bit of a laugh. To be honest, we are both pretty rubbish at it, much to Dad's dismay."

"I take your bad and double it. I'm useless at this game."

"Ah, don't overthink it. We're just here to have a bit of fun."

I nod.

"Robby says he'll be here in ten minutes."

"That means he hasn't left home yet," Leo chirps. "I say, let's start and put the flake on caddy duty when he finally arrives."

Leo didn't exaggerate. Robby arrived an hour later without an apology or the slightest haste in his step. He also wasn't dressed for golf, wearing his baggy jeans and hoodie. And the man bun in the hair just underlined his laid-back vibe.

"You started without me!" he greets us from the far end of the green.

The brothers greet each other with a one-arm hug and slaps on the back. No one seems in the least fussed that Robby is late. Father and son kiss each other on the cheek.

"You must be Adam. Hi there, brother," he greets me and catches me unawares when he pulls me into a hug.

"Not much of a hugger, eh?"

Before I can utter a response, Robert interrupts, "Make yourself useful and pass me the nine iron."

Robby complies with an exaggerated sigh. "Golf, such fun."

I reflect on these young men. So different from me. So relaxed in their own skin. And I realise this is what I've been missing out on: the steadfast sense of belonging that allows you that kind of freedom to find yourself without any pressure to conform. A deep sense of sadness takes hold of me. No envy, but sorrow. It is possible to miss things you've never had.

Despite my best attempts to stay aloof, the lads include me in their jokes. Each takes turns telling me embarrassing stories about the other. And I find myself laughing and enjoying their company.

"Oh, God, do you remember that time we went camping and Robby farted like twenty times in the space of a minute and nearly suffocated us all?"

Robert starts laughing so hard, that the tears start running down his cheeks.

"Ah," says Robby in his best storytelling voice, "it was the summer of 2006. I was just a wee lad of fifteen…"

"Your mother nearly killed you," Robert reminds him. We all laugh.

"Scottish Dave, a guy in my squad, he's a beast with an appetite to match. He will eat anything and everything. On my last tour," I start telling them, and I see that they have all stopped whatever they were busy with to listen to me. I clear my throat, uncomfortable holding their attention like this.

"…On my last tour, we got sent to a village in Nahr-e Saraj. It's mud huts and goats tied to trees. We have…had a clinic there…. Anyway, the locals sometimes make big pots of food and share them with us. But eating it is a bit of a gamble, and more times than not, it'll have you shitting through the eye of a needle for days afterwards if you do. We tell Scottish Dave to stay away from the food because the latrines are nasty at the best of times, and believe me, you don't want to get stuck in there."

Roberts senior and junior and Leo are chuckling good-heartedly at my rendition of the incident, charmingly bemused by my outlandish army tale.

"He ate from the pot?" Leo prods me to go on.

"Well, yeah. He took it as a challenge." I shake my head. "It ended badly. The guys accused him of eating rats he stank so much."

More laughter.

"Did he get the shits?" Robby asks. "And then what happened?"

I open my mouth to speak and shut it abruptly. I can't be telling this story. Not *this* story.

All three look at me expectantly.

"Sorry. This is a terrible story. I shouldn't be telling it."

I'm out of place here. I don't belong with these people. Even my attempt to join in with a funny story is a fucking disaster.

"Actually, I shouldn't even be here." I drop my putter into the bag and swing it onto my shoulder. I take no more than three steps when Robert calls after me.

"Hey, where are you going?"

I turn to him; exasperated, I throw my arms wide. "What do you want from me, Robert? I don't belong here. Do you know how the story ends? My best friend ends up

204

with a bullet in his chest while his patrol partner had to find a bush to shit in."

Silence.

"Yeah." I turn to go.

"Stay," Robert says to my back. "Son, I'm asking you to stay."

I don't turn to stay, but also don't take another step. I feel him close in, and it makes me want to run. Then he gently rests his hand on my shoulder.

"What was your friend's name?"

"Pete," I whisper, and saying his name makes the lump in my throat thick. I'm finding it hard to take in air.

"I'm sorry you lost your friend. Truly I am. But if you walk away from us, your family, we'll be missing out on the opportunity to be here for you. And we want that. We want to be here for you, Adam."

I don't register that I had closed my eyes, but when I open them, Leo and Robby have joined the makeshift circle. They don't say anything but nod in agreement with their dad. My dad too, I realise.

"Shall we give this a skip and head straight for the nineteenth hole?" Robert asks.

I nod.

"Yeah, I'm starved. I haven't eaten since yesterday, I think," Robby confesses.

I give him a quizzical look.

"Professional game tester slash developer means that sometimes whole days are lost to me."

"Only salad for me," Leo chimes in. "I have a shoot in the morning. I don't want to be bloated."

"What is it exactly you do?"

"I'm an actor slash producer. Shooting a commercial tomorrow."

"Right," I say, shaking my head. How different can our day-to-day be?

"I could actually use a consultant on this TV series I'm co-producing. Your military knowledge will go a long way in helping us get the army stuff right in the show."

"Sure," I say.

We start walking to the clubhouse.

"Not for free, obviously. I'll bring you in as a consultant."

"Leo, I'm happy to help you out, no charge. Seriously."

"No way, man. That would not be fair. We pay all other consultants, and the money isn't bad."

"Yeah, but I'm not a consultant. I'm not even sure I can do what you need?"

"Sure you can. Give me your number, and we'll do lunch sometime and I'll explain everything to you then."

"Okay."

He flashes me one of his brilliant smiles. The guy is a pretty boy, but he is so damn nice, it's hard to dislike him.

I glance at Robert who gives me a wink.

"We want to hear all about Evie and the baby," Robert tells me.

I smile. That's a topic I can talk about all day.

EIGHTEEN

EVIE

"OKAY, OPEN THEM."

Adam is standing behind me with his hands covering my eyes. I was told to close my eyes the moment the car turned into the driveway.

We've just made the long journey home, the car stuffed with even more than I left with. But with just four weeks until my due date, and Christmas two weeks away, it was the right time to come back. Home. To Adam and our new life as a family.

When I open my eyes, I screech with pure joy. Adam has painted the front door bright red and has wrapped fairy lights around the pillars of the little porch. It's magical and perfect.

"Your mum made the wreath," he tells me.

I turn to him and wrap my arms around his neck.

"Adam Taylor, how did I get so lucky to find a guy like you?"

He kisses me deeply, but we're interrupted by Fosters' frantic barking by the living room window.

"I know of someone else who's also happy you're home."

"I thought she was at my mum's!"

"I asked her to bring her back in time for our arrival."

"Are you telling me you gave my mum a key before you gave me one?"

He slips his hand into his coat pocket and pulls out a freshly cut silver key.

"Only out of necessity," he assures me with a cheeky grin as he hands me the key.

"You do know she will never let me forget how she got keys first, right?"

"Oh yeah," he nods.

Adam won't let me lift a finger with the unloading of the car, so the belly and I end up lying on the sofa with Fosters.

"That's it. Damn, woman. Did you have to try and bring all of Bruges with you?"

"Nope, just the best parts. God, I can't believe I have to pee again."

"You're adorable when you waddle to the toilet."

"Ugh."

"Just saying. I'll get the fire going, it's cold in here."

I'm about to abuse my pregnant woman's powers and demand a cup of tea for the Bean, when I realise I've wet myself.

"Aww, shit! I've wet myself!"

Adam is with me within a nanosecond. He looks at the puddle on the floor and then at me. I've started giggly nervously, embarrassed by the indignity of it all.

"Darling, you didn't pee yourself. I think your waters just broke."

ADAM

"IT'S TOO SOON! Isn't it too soon?" Evie's eyes are wide.

"Thirty-six weeks and four days..." I scour my brain for all my newly learnt pregnancy knowledge. "Thirty-six weeks is term." Barely. But I don't say that. "Do you have any cramps?"

"Well, I had some cramps earlier when we stopped at the rest station, but I thought it was from the curry."

"Why didn't you tell me? You were already in labour! How long ago was that?"

"I don't know. An hour ago? Hour and a half?"

"It's okay, we've got time. Let's get you cleaned up, then I'll phone the hospital. And your mum."

As if on cue, Evie doubles over, well as much as you can with a beachball where your stomach should be, and groans. I check my watch and start timing the contractions.

The pain lasts for about half a minute.

"Are you okay?"

"Mm-mm," she says followed by, "Oh crap! I don't

even have the hospital bag packed yet. And the room. We haven't even set up her room, Adam!"

"Follow me," I say, and I lead her upstairs. I open the spare bedroom door with a flourish and flip the light switch.

"I think the room is nearly done though," I say, unable to suppress my pride in my achievement. I worked late most nights to get the room done. Floors, paint job, changing station and cot and mobile were all ready.

"Adam." She walks up to the cot and runs her hands along the polished grain of the oak. "You did this?"

"Surprise," I say softly, not wanting to break the spell of Evie's wonder.

"Mermaid curtains!"

"Ah, your mum's handiwork, as well as the bedding."

I join her in the middle of the room, pulling her close to me so that my arms encircle her from behind. Even though she's literally about to pop, I can still reach all the way around.

"I take it you approve?"

"I definitely do."

"I think your mum filled the drawers of this chest with at least one of everything she could find at Pappa's and Mamma's. Tell me what to throw in the bag and I'll do that while you shower."

Evie laughs. "You mean Mamma's and Pappa's?"

"Sure."

Evie makes a list, and I pack the bag while she showers. When she starts drying herself off, she stops and holds her breath as the next contraction hits.

I check my watch. "That's eighteen minutes since the last one. I'll call the hospital and let them know."

She nods and sits on the edge of the bed while she recovers.

"They say we should come when the contractions are ten minutes apart. What a load of horse shit! What in the hell do they expect us to do until then?"

"Drink tea? Watch a movie? Tell me you bought a TV?"

I shake my head. "Tea it is, then."

The bag stands ready at the door. Evie paces the kitchen, anticipating the next wave of pain and when it hits, she hisses through her teeth and puts on the bravest face I've ever seen. We spend another two hours drinking tea, listening to music, and playing Bananagrams. And then it's time.

We arrive at the hospital, and at first, everything seems to happen too slowly for my liking. The paperwork is taking too long, and they are taking forever to assess Evie, who's crying out in agony every few minutes. But then she's taken into the room for her examination, and the rest is a blur of hurried nurses and a midwife calling orders.

Give me defusing bombs any day over watching the woman I love cry out in pain over and over again. When Evie pushes and the sinew in her delicate neck becomes rope-like and her face looks like it's going to explode, I want to carry her off the birthing table and take her anywhere that isn't here.

The midwife keeps telling her that she's doing well, but it sure as shit doesn't look like it. More than once they've had to bring her back from unconsciousness between contractions and instruct her to push again. She keeps passing out from the pain.

"Isn't there anything you can do for her? An epidural?" I'm desperate to save her the agony of bringing our child into the world.

"It's too late for that now."

For some reason, I thought my job would be to pass her ice chips and cheer her on. But in here I'm as useless as the nipples on a Batman suit. She doesn't squeeze my hand; instead, she grips the edge of the bed until her knuckles go white and then she passes out.

"Jesus Christ! Isn't there anything you can do for her? How much longer can she carry on like this?"

I get ignored, and we go through another round of Evie being brought to, only to have her push again.

One of the Jamaican nurses wipes Evie's brow with a cold cloth and speaks to her softly.

"C'mom now, Mamma, you got this. One more big push. One more."

Evie gives it her all, and fifteen minutes later, our baby slips into the world.

"Is it a girl? Why isn't she crying?" Evie goes from curious to concerned in less than a second.

"It's a girl," the consultant announces, and at the same time, we hear a sneeze and get the confirmation that our daughter is perfectly healthy.

"Not all babies come out wailing; some sneeze to tell us their airways are open and working just fine."

I cut the umbilical cord, and when they place our tiny, perfect human in my big, old, clumsy hands, I'm terrified and elated in a single moment. I pass her to her mamma, who immediately holds her to her chest and starts talking to her.

"Hello. Hello, little one. Welcome to the world," she whispers.

NINETEEN

EVIE

FOR A PRECIOUS HOUR after Stella's arrival into the world, Adam and I are left alone with our little miracle. Adam sidles up close to me on the hospital bed, unable to take his eyes off his daughter's face. My heart is so full, I could burst with love for my baby and Adam right beside me.

"Thank you," he whispers, before giving me a kiss on the forehead. I know he means thank you for Stella.

"You made her too," I remind him, but she shakes his head and tells me she's perfect because she's all me.

"I love you," I tell him.

"I love you, Evie."

Once we're home, everyone comes to meet Stella. Adam and I choose the name together because it sounds like "stellar" and this girl is our perfect star.

Mum and Dad bring more gifts. Gerald brings

flowers and his new beau and makes me laugh so hard with his coming-out story that I'm sure I pull a stitch. Adam and I ask him to be Stella's godfather, and he readily agrees, as long as we add "fairy" to the title.

Patty and Robert make the drive from Sheffield to come and see their first grandchild. The discomfort of having these strangers be part of our family lasts only as long as it takes for Stella to land in Grandma Patty's arms.

"Here we are darling," Adam says to me as we pull into the drive.

I carry Stella in my arms and introduce Fosters to the new member of her pack.

LATER THAT NIGHT, Adam and I sit on the sofa, watching the newly installed TV while I feed Stella.

"You can go to bed, you know. It's not like you can help me with this."

"Never. Who knows when I'll be able to see your boobs this huge again."

I swat him with a muslin cloth. "You're the worst, you know that? Go make yourself useful and bring me a glass of water, please."

"Yes, ma'am."

"ARE you sure you're going to be alright?" After three days of leave, Adam has to head back to work.

"No," I tell him. And I mean it.

"Your mum will be here by nine-thirty. It's two hours. You'll be fine," he reassures me.

"What if she stops breathing?" I'm starting to whine, and I hate myself in this moment.

"Keep the baby monitor with you."

"What if she chokes?" I insist on my train of 'all the bad things that can happen' thoughts.

"Did your breast milk suddenly become lumpy?" Adam tries to make light, but I'm not having it.

"No!"

"C'mon, darling. You got this. I'll be home by six."

I walk into him, like I always do, and instantly his arms encircle me.

"This is why I need you here. I'm freaking out," I tell him.

He kisses the top of my head. "Do you trust me?"

"Of course."

"Then trust me when I tell you that you are a fantastic mamma, okay?"

I nod, feeling slightly more confident in my ability to survive at least until my mum gets here.

Adam kisses 'his girls' goodbye; I stand at the window and watch Fosters walk him to the gate. I smile when I watch him say goodbye to the dog before she turns and gallops on her three good legs back to the house.

With Mum's help, I manage to shove the lasagne she brought into the oven and shower and change into fresh pyjamas before Adam comes home.

"Honey, you're home!" I call to him, referencing the TV show *Dinosaurs* we used to watch way back when.

He's come in, taken off his beret, and not yet met my eyes.

"Adam, what's the matter?"

He pulls me close and kisses my forehead before he speaks. "I got notice of my deployment just as I was leaving to come home."

"What? They're deploying you with just fourteen weeks left on your contract?"

"They can and they are."

"Bastards!" I yell, pulling loose from him and stomping away.

"Evie...it's okay. It's just three months. Mostly training."

"Where?"

He hesitates for too long and then I know it's Afghan.

"Don't cry, darling, please. You're making this harder," he pleads with me. But I can't stop the tears because I'm hormonal and sleep-deprived and I don't want him to die and make me a widow before I even marry him.

"When do you leave?"

Once again, Adam hesitates, and my brief recess of tears is ambushed by my emotions that open the flood gates to more tears. I see the pained look in his eyes. I see the anguish behind the tightness around his mouth, and I know I shouldn't make this more difficult for him, but I just can't. There is much more at stake now. On cue, Stella starts crying, but neither of us move to comfort her.

I take a deep breath, and although my voice is shaky, I manage to ask him again, more gently this time. "Just tell me. When do you have to go?"

"It hasn't been finalised yet, but it looks like just after Christmas."

Stella's persistent crying makes my breasts ache, and I notice that I've started lactating, as my T-shirt is wet. Adam steps closer, ignoring the indignity of my weeping breasts, and pulls me close and holds me.

Encircled in his arms, strong and secure around me, I feel safe. I feel like I am home. He is my home. For a minute we stay this way, and then he steps back.

"Let me run you a bath. I'll feed Stella. Did you manage to express today?" he asks, his voice steady and gentle.

I nod.

"Good." He plants a kiss on my forehead before making his way to our little girl. I watch him lean over the Moses basket next to the sofa and I hear him whisper something to Stella before he cradles her. Like me, she's instantly soothed by him. He turns and smiles at me, before taking Stella upstairs to run my bath.

I watch him disappear up the stairs and my heart breaks a little. I try to commit this tender moment with Stella to memory, hoping that one day I won't have to relay stories and anecdotes about how much her father loved her—that she will experience all of it first-hand.

I AM grateful that we can have Christmas together. Adam brought his record player along, and the whole family is listening to Michael Bublé croon the carols and songs we know well enough to sing along to.

Daddy has found his jovial spirit—mainly whiskey—and Mum is drinking so much fizz, she already has the hiccups. She and Patty are wearing Christmas-themed aprons and preparing the food side by side for the big feast tomorrow. It's like a Hallmark movie but I'm too happy to care how corny my family is.

Adam's parents have joined us for Christmas Eve canapés and Adam's brothers will join us for the big lunch tomorrow. It feels surreal. Everything I ever wanted is happening right now. Our family has grown to include siblings and a child of our own, our world is bigger and so much more beautiful for it. But in the back of my mind, Adam's imminent deployment to the Afghanistan war zone threatens our newfound status quo as a family.

Adam hands me a cup of tea. I'm sitting on the sofa, cradling Stella with Fosters at my feet. Even the dog hasn't escaped Mum's incessant need to decorate absolutely everything, as she's wearing her own obligatory Christmas jumper. It was impossible to deny Mum's insistence on Fosters' jumper when she had knitted it herself, making sure it only had three openings for her legs.

"Daddy's turn," Adam says, extending his arms to receive his baby girl. She accepts his warmth without a fuss.

One day I'm going to paint a picture of this moment. I want to capture the deep-rooted joy on Adam's face, the soft creases around his eyes as he smiles at his sleeping daughter.

He turns to me, a wide lovestruck grin on his face. "Hey, what are you doing?"

"Taking a photo," I say, casually putting my mobile away. I lean over and kiss him.

"Your mum did a great job with the tree this year," Adam says.

"You do know that most of the packages under there are for Stella. Even though she isn't even aware what Christmas is yet."

Adam chuckles. "Yeah, this beautiful girl is everyone's darling."

"We should probably put her down upstairs and join the party," I suggest.

"In a bit. I just want to hold her a little longer." He gives me a pained look, and I know where his mind is, and it breaks my heart.

In less than a week, Adam has to deploy to Afghan for three months. Now that he has found his parents and Stella is here, I'm not sure my soldier's heart can bear to be away from his little girl.

"I'm going to take good care of her, Adam. You just have to focus on coming back to us. We'll be here. I promise."

He nods and pulls Stella closer for a kiss on the head.

After Stella is put down for a couple of hours, Adam and I join the party downstairs. Daddy insists we all stay awake until midnight. And looking at the state of the grandparents and the empty bottles, I'm glad we're all sleeping over.

"Seriously, Daddy, I'm ready for bed. I have about

three hours before your granddaughter will want to be fed. Can we get this show on the road?"

"Alright, alright. No need to be such a party pooper."

"Pooper!" Mum calls out before she blows on her party horn and the green and red foil unfurls in a hooooooooot.

This makes Patty laugh so hard she almost spills her Cabernet Sauvignon on the beige carpet.

"Mummy, have you been naughty or nice?" Daddy teases Mum. Adam and I exchange cringes at the innuendo.

But Mum plays along and giggles like a schoolgirl.

By the shape of the box, it's definitely jewellery and I have no doubt that she chose it herself just days ago.

"And what do we have here? Eve, it's for you. Such a small box. I wonder what it could be."

I gulp. Adam drops his gaze, suddenly shy.

"Adam, I believe you should be the one to give this to Eve."

Adam takes the box from my father and comes to sit beside me on the floor.

I pull off the paper and sit and stare at the velvet, domed box.

"Open it," Adam encourages me.

Everyone has gone quiet.

I open it, my eyes immediately fill with tears.

"I love you. Thank you for giving me our daughter. She is the best gift. And you—you are amazing, my love."

"They're beautiful," I muster, and I show everyone in the room the diamond earrings in the box.

Mum is the first to recover. "That's beautiful, darling."

"Yes, yes, " Patty agrees, "very pretty."

I don't look up to see my father's face.

"Well, " I say with strained cheerfulness. "That's me! Off to bed now."

I walk away as fast as I can, but I hear Daddy say, "What a bloody idiot."

ADAM

THIS IS THE HARDEST GOODBYE.

Evie cradles Stella in her pink cocoon. She's swaddled in a pink fleece blanket up to her chin, beanie pulled down low over her forehead—a porcelain doll with her perfect, heart-shaped lips and rosy cheeks. I hold onto my little family a little longer, even though I know I'll be collected any minute now. I want to hold onto this feeling of having them safely in my embrace. I want to remember Stella's sweet baby breath and Evie's scent. But eventually, it's time and I have to go. I step back and clear my throat.

"Darling."

"Don't say anything. You're just going to work, right? We'll see you for dinner...in three months' time."

For my sake, she cracks a smile and blinks away the tears threatening to fall.

Fosters nuzzles her face against my legs and I bend down to pat her head. "You better take care of my girls, okay?" I look into Fosters' eyes; she knows where I'm going. She knows because she's been there. She answers our wordless exchange with a small whimper, and I hug her tightly.

"One more mission," Evie tells me with firm resolve in her voice.

I nod.

The beeping of the car horn of my lift to the base means it's time for me to go. I kiss her goodbye and tell her I love her.

"I'm coming home to you, Evie Simpson. Don't you dare forget it."

I turn round one last time and wave before I get into the car with the lads. When the cottage is out of sight, I tap my breast pocket and feel the shape of the ring with which I intend to ask Evie to marry me. It's my talisman. Knowing it's there, that she's waiting for me and that our future will be together, will get me through the coming months.

———

AT THE BASE, we load up onto the bus that will take us to the airport. All the lads are there. Devereaux and Little jog up to me and give me a hug when they see me. Scottish Dave waits until I give a nod, and then we shake hands.

"Staff, I just want to say—"

I cut him off. "No need, MacGill. This is the military. Shit happens. Let's just leave it at that. I'm glad you're here."

"Staff, this is Sergeant Cameron, our new dog handler." Captain Meyer has joined the circle of uniforms around me.

I extend my hand to Cameron, who is a short and stocky bloke with a smile that should be on a toothpaste advertisement.

"This is Bulmer," he tells me, pointing to the German shepherd obediently sitting at his heels.

Bulmer looks a lot like Fosters did before her amputation. Although he is a bit heavier.

"We had a shepherd on the team called Fosters before... What is it with handlers naming their dogs after whatever's on tap at the pub?"

Cameron laughs. "'Tis true. My last dog was called Jager."

I shake my head. "Well, it's nice to have you both." I call Devereaux. "Make Cameron feel welcome and introduce him to everyone, will you?"

"Yes, Staff."

When the gathering moves to another huddle of men a few feet away, the captain turns to me. "How are you feeling, Dickens?"

"Good, sir. Good."

"This is your last tour, Staff, so make it a good one. And let's bring these boys home safe 'n sound."

I hear what he's saying even though he hasn't said it.

"How bad is it?"

The captain keeps his eyes fixed in the distance. "Let's just say things are heating up."

TWENTY

ADAM

AS SOON AS I break my jump out of the chinook with my hand and I come into contact with the damp, rough earth, I know that I'm a million miles away from home. We've got a two-mile march to Bastion, so I rally the squad around me for further instructions.

"We march north, along the river bed. Single file. Cameron, you take the back. Little, Devereaux, you're up front with me. We are going to keep the pace steady. No chitty-chatting and fart-arsing around. Stay quiet. We don't need any attention from the Terry's. Got it? Let's go!"

We walk in single file. I imagine we look like ants with the bags on our backs looking like humps. We're wearing our combat gear, so that means helmets for the army ants.

When we reach the safety of the camp, I give Devereaux a slap between the shoulder blades.

"I see you didn't let your mother pack for you this time, eh?"

"Haha." Devereaux blushes from the roots of his hair down to the collar of his shirt.

"I'm glad you're here, man. Pete and I...I mean Sergeant Anderson and I were really worried about you on your first tour."

Devereaux nods. "There were days I didn't think I would make it out of here alive... I'm sorry about Pete, Staff, he was a good guy."

The grief I thought I had already unpacked and folded and put away in its own box, shows its ugly head again and has me wiping at my leaky eyes.

Little joins us. Oblivious to the emotional current, he defuses the build-up and saves us from breaching the unwritten rule that men don't cry.

"Is it true that Lieutenant Janssen and her squadron are here? Do you think they brought those Dutch-ball thingies with them?"

"If it's true, I want to speak to her." I walk in the direction of the Ops tent to get more information.

"Staff!" Little calls, "don't forget about the balls!"

"Hey, Little!" I yell back, "grow a pair!"

I find Katja on the outskirts of the camp. She and her team have come to return the favour of the training we only half gave them, by coming to demonstrate some new pieces of artillery their army has bought in.

She's alone. As a woman, she'll only share sleeping quarters with other women, but since she's technically a guest, and I assume there are no other free beds, she's been given her own space. I have to wonder if this is a perk or if it makes her life in the army just that much more lonely.

"Knock, knock," I say at the entrance.

Her face breaks into a smile when she sees me, and because there's no one around, we break protocol and hug each other. Despite being little more than acquaintances, I feel like we'll always be bonded by our memories of Pete.

"How are you?" I ask.

"I'm doing okay, actually. Counting down the days until I leave this place. You?"

"Same. Evie had the baby. We called her Stella." I pull out my favourite photo of my daughter so far.

Katja studies the photo and smiles. "She looks like you."

"God, I hope not." I chuckle, trying to hide my pride.

"Do you know what you'll be doing next?" I ask. It's my dilemma too. While working in the military teaches you some incredible skills, not many of them translate well in the real world.

"Close protection, maybe?" She says, "I have a friend in London who says I can stay with her. I might do that. You?"

"My brother," I say, trying the word out loud for the first time and it feels right and good, "works in film and says he can bring me in as a consultant for some of the films. You know, making sure they get the action scenes right. He's one of the producers for a new military TV show."

"Sounds cushy."

"Yeah, I'm all in for cushy. I want to be home for my family."

She nods. "So you've asked Evie to marry you?"

I sigh. "I really wanted to at Christmas. Had the ring and everything. But it just didn't feel right."

I dig into my breast pocket and retrieve the princess-cut diamond set in a white-gold band. I show it to her.

"What do you think?"

"Honestly?"

"Of course."

"I think you're a complete *domkop* for not asking her sooner."

I don't need to ask what the word means; I guess it means idiot. "Fair enough, Lieutenant, fair enough," I concede.

When our weak laughter fades, I put a hand on her shoulder. "I want you to know that I'm here if you need anything. And if you do find yourself in England, look me up. Come visit us."

"I will. Thank you."

I nod.

"Beer?" she asks.

"Tea. But yeah, let's grab something to eat, as well. It's been a long day. I don't suppose—"

"I swear, if another British soldier asks me about *bitterballen*, I'm going to lose it. So just don't."

"Copy that, Lieutenant."

"HI, DARLING." There's a subtle lag on the satellite phone we have to use for our weekly fifteen-minute 'morale' calls.

In the background, I can hear Stella wailing.

"Is everything okay? Is this a bad time?" Instinctively, I check my watch to calculate the time difference. It's 5 pm in the UK, the torturous suicide hour with infants who tend to really test their lungs and voices at hour.

"Gimme a sec," I hear Evie sshhh, sshhh Stella. "Here you go," she says to her.

"Okay, I'm back. How much time do we have left?"

"Thirteen minutes," I tell her. "Is she being fussy?"

Evie lets out a long sigh. "Nope, she's just hungry again. I feel like all I do is feed her, change her, bath her, rock her to sleep." She yawns. "Enough about the pyjama drill. Tell me about the Afghan drill."

Since I can't tell her about any of the missions or the fact that tomorrow, at dawn the squad and I are being choppered to an undisclosed location for some serious work, I tell her about seeing Katja again.

"She's also leaving the army. Going into Close Protection services."

"Is that something you'd like to do?" she asks me, knowing full well I'm not fully sold on the idea of relying on my newfound sibling for a job.

"I haven't really considered it. The idea of the consultancy with Leo is growing on me," I admit. "I think I can even rope in some vets to work for me."

"That's smart thinking, darling." Another extended yawn from Evie.

"You sound tired."

"Uh-ha. I am. Little Miss Sunshine here has her days and nights mixed up. And do you know what the biggest load of crap ever is?"

"Tell me."

"Sleep when the baby sleeps. Ha! Babies don't sleep for longer than an hour at a time. Max two hours. How the hell does that work then?"

"Oh, darling. Maybe you should go to your parents this weekend and catch up on some Zs."

"Mum's fetching me tomorrow. I can't wait till the weekend."

"Good. Good. And how's my other girl?"

"You mean my shadow? She's great. The only sane one left in the house actually. She sleeps in front of the crib when I have to put Stella down when I shower."

A static pause.

"Darling? I have to go now, but I just wanted to say I love you. And I'll call you next week, okay?"

The silence lasts so long that I'm about to hang up, thinking we've lost connection.

"You're about to do something very dangerous, aren't you?" she murmurs.

"Evie..."

"I know you can't say anything. But listen to me, Adam Taylor. You'd better get that sexy arse of yours home. I need you here. Stella needs you. Hell, even Fosters could do with her dad around. Don't take any chances, okay? Be safe."

"I'll be safe. I promise." My hand instinctively goes to the pocket where the ring lies waiting. I feel it there and it gives me the resolve I need. I can't guarantee I won't take any chances. This is a war zone, and sometimes a chance is all you have to save yourself.

MY FAMILIAR FRIEND Unease comes and settles inside me while we fly high above the craggy mountains of Afghanistan. It's Nahr-e Saraj all over again, except it's a different village, and this time the insurgents opened fire in a mosque. It makes no sense. But then, none of this does. Our squad, callsign METALHEAD 14 has been brought in to sweep the area. And we've been told that we can expect to find plenty.

I slip my hand into my man bag and start feeling around for all my tools. When I'm satisfied they are all there in their correct places, I sit and observe the rest. Little, who really doesn't do well in the air, is green at the gills, and he sits with his head hung between his knees. Devereaux is hard to read. His expression gives nothing away, and he, like me, sits clutching the bag. Scottish Dave lies with his head back, pretending to sleep. Cameron makes eye contact with me and gives me a nod. Bulmer lies between his legs, and he strokes him every few minutes to keep him calm, and possibly himself, too. Our two newest members are Privates Peters and Smit, the latter already dubbed Gaz because his first name is Gavin.

I glance out of the window. A brilliant red sea of poppies stands out against the harsh, dull, orange earth. All that opium farmed for just one reason, to keep the Taliban army high. The view would be breathtaking if it wasn't so tragic.

We get dropped just one mile from the village and hike the rest of the way. It's easy terrain, for the most part, and we cover the distance in twelve minutes without pushing hard. I leave the men to orientate themselves with our other troops who are stationed there, while I receive further instructions.

Captain Rodrigues and I greet each other formally by rank and a salute, and I wait for the invitation to be seated. It doesn't come. So I stand at ease, looking past the commander. He doesn't have to invite me to take a seat, and I don't have to make eye contact.

"Let me get straight to the point, Staff. The last few days have been a shit show. It's raining brass and we don't see the storm clouds coming. Now there are some abandoned buildings not too far away. We expect this is where they're fudging the IEDs. We've had two bombs go off. Fortunately not in the village yet—just gunfire. But we suspect they're sending us a message. Our intel strongly suggests that they're planning to plant IEDs."

"We'll start with sweeping the buildings and take it from there."

"Staff!"

I drop my gaze to meet his eyes for the first time since our greeting.

"We have schools here for the village kids. Many of them orphaned or abandoned. Some of the factions have threatened the students and teachers, saying the school is secular and not in line with their beliefs. Meanwhile, the teachers are devout Muslims and are simply teaching and distributing food brought in by the British army, for God's sake!" The captain slams his fist on the table, and two pens, in hiding under some scattered papers, roll onto the floor.

"Then we should start with the school and have one of our squad stationed there for eyes and ears, doing regular sweeps."

"Very good."

He sits down with heavy bones and the chair legs shift against the wooden floorboards to accommodate his bulk. The man is weary. Wrung out like an overused cloth that's been left to dry in the wind and sun. The creases on his face will never be smoothed out again.

I watch him while I wait for him to add to his instructions. But nothing comes. When he looks up again, he seems surprised to find me still standing there.

"Dismissed!"

I nod and turn on my heel, grateful that I'll be free before all the life is squeezed out of me.

I INSTRUCT the men to do a thorough sweep of the school and beyond the perimeter. Six metal detectors and Bulmer get to work. One by one, they all come and report the all-clear to me.

"Where's Scottish Dave?"

The men look at each other. No one knows.

"For fuck's sake!" I drop my cigarette to the ground and stamp on the lit end with the heel of my boot. I leave the guys behind and go look for MacGill. I walk around the makeshift building that's half-crumbling brick and half-corrugated iron sheets, stabilised with not much more than bricks on the roof and at the corners. Rusty corners poke out, and I wonder how the kids manage to stay safe here. But then it's still safer in there than out on the streets.

"MacGill!" I yell, and I hope my frustration follows through in my voice and makes him move his humongous arse faster. "I swear to God, if you don't get here by the count of five, I'm making you do drills without dinner! One! Two!"

"Staff!"

I stop when I hear MacGill's voice. I have no idea where it's coming from.

"Here!" he calls again. Why does he sound so far away?

Beyond the perimeter we swept, is an old shed. If I'm right, Scottish Dave is in there. I break into a run, immediately sensing something's horribly wrong.

I call him as I approach. And then I hear whimpering.

The door is open but MacGill stops me in my tracks. "Don't come any closer. We have a situation."

My eyes adjust from the harsh sunlight to the dim room. Dust and chicken shit aggravate my nostrils, and I end up coughing into my elbow. And then I see it. MacGill is on his knees, his cricket-mitt hands covering the hands of a boy no older than six or seven. The boy is holding an empty plastic bottle with a bomb in it. Spider-like wires protrude at various angles.

"He told me he thought it was a spaceship. He wants to let it go, but..."

The boy starts crying.

"It's okay. It's okay. Let me take a look." I'm speaking to the child but it's MacGill that nods.

I step closer, suddenly painfully aware that my reinforced uniform doesn't stand a chance against an IED. The last time I wore a full bomb suit was in training. But with lugging a backpack of fifty-plus kilos and the heavy uniform on the body, there's no way any of us can wear a bomb suit in these temperatures. It's just not practical. But they don't tell you that in training. Instead, they let you make the choice. Haha. The joke's on us.

I inspect the bottle.

"The detonator is in the bottle, Staff," Scottish Dave reaffirms what I'm seeing.

The bomb is a monster in a see-through cage. I'm awestruck and terrified all in one breath.

"Geesus. They constructed this thing like those ships in a bottle."

Scottish Dave has fear vibrating from every pore, and I see how his hands are starting to shake.

"Can you hold it for a bit longer?" I ask him even though there can only be one answer. Still, I do it so that he feels he's in control. It's a bullshit bit of psychology they teach you, but since I've got nothing else to motivate him to hold on, I use it. And then he calls me on it.

"Do I have a choice?"

I ignore him. My brain is firing fast and I need to get to work even faster.

"Here's what we're going to do."

I relay my plan to run back and tell everyone to clear the area. I'll bring just one other member of the squad with me: Little. He's the nimblest of the squad and I'll need him to move fast once we've extracted the boy. Our priority is to get the child out. And then, I'll slice a square out of the top of the bottle. After that...

MacGill loosens his grip on the kid's hands, and I hold his wrists steady as I slide his hands out. Beads of sweat gather on the Scotsman's brow as we both hold our breath, anticipating the worst. When we succeed, I waste no time and pass the boy over to Little, who tucks him under his arm like a rugby ball and runs to safety.

Then the real work starts. I use a scalpel from my medical kit and take my time making the hole I need. When it's done, I look to Scottish Dave.

"Nearly there, buddy. Nearly there."

He nods, his eyes not blinking, just staring at the block of soft plasticine now exposed. I use the tweezers, also from the first aid box, and gently separate the wires.

"Okay, MacGill. Listen to me. I can't see under this thing, so we have to assume it's got a second detonator. That means I'm going to clip the wires. Okay?"

Dave doesn't answer. "MacGill, say okay if you're hearing me."

"Okay," he says.

"Good. After I clip the wires, we're going to gently put this on the floor and run like hell. Got it?"

He nods.

I snip the wires. Then I place my hands over his, just like he did with the child. And we keep eye contact while we gently lower the sleeping monster to the ground. Once my hands are off his, he lets go, and we both turn to run. We know we have no more than five seconds to get away as far as we can. I count the seconds.

TWO.

THREE.

I look over my shoulder and see Dave fall over his own feet.

FIVE.

"Fuck!" I yell as I dive away from the blast.

When I lift my head out of the gravel, I see the squad running towards me with fire extinguishers. I hear MacGill howl. Somehow, I'm back on my feet and running towards the flames. The last second, before I pass through the ring of fire imprisoning Dave, Evie and Stella's smiling faces flash before my eyes.

TWENTY-ONE

EVIE

IT'S the end of April. I cross another day off the calendar. It's my countdown until Adam's homecoming. Just two months more to go. It's a useful but also dangerous coping mechanism. At first, I measure the time remaining in months because six months sounds more manageable than one hundred and eight-two days. But when we're down to one-and-a-half months, I start counting the days down from fifty. It's my little game and it keeps me sane. But while it does the job of making me feel like the end is in sight, it also sets the expectation that he will be home on a given date. And if there's one thing I've learned about the army, assumption makes an ass of you and me.

I look over at the clock on the wall, and realise I've nearly run out of time. Patsy is coming to visit. She's been making an effort to come and see Stella and me every couple of weeks—visits I've come to look forward to.

Getting to know Adam's mum, seeing how much like her he is, despite having never grown up under her influence, still astounds me. There's a lot to be said for nature versus nurture.

Right on time Patsy pulls up onto the gravel drive, and immediately Fosters is on her feet and whining at the back door to be let out. I open it for her, and she trots over to greet the familiar human she, too, has gotten to know. I watch Patsy talk to Fosters and scratch her behind the ears before she looks up in my direction and gives me a bright smile and a wave. I shake my head when I see she's carrying another bag which I can only assume, based on past visits, either contains a homemade meal or a gift for Stella or both.

"You really don't have to come bearing gifts every single time," I scold her, as I pull her into a hug.

"How are you?" Patsy replies, ignoring my gentle admonishment.

I pull away from her, and place my hands on both of her shoulders and take a sterner approach. "I'm serious. You don't have to. You're welcome here anytime—without gifts!"

I'm unprepared for the tears that fill her eyes, and I immediately pull her right back to me and hold her.

"What's the matter?" I ask. She doesn't answer me right away, but when she does, there's so much raw emotion in her eyes and her voice, that it breaks my heart.

"It's just..." She dabs a tissue systematically from the inner corner of her eye to the outer, drying her tears. "...It's just that I'm so grateful to be in your and Adam's lives. I lost a son, and now I not only have him

239

back, I'm blessed with a daughter and granddaughter, too."

Her tears are contagious, and I feel my heart swell with a genuine love for her.

"Oh, Patsy..." But before we can both start blubbering all over again, Stella lets out a wail which tells me she's woken from her nap, likely wet or dirty or both.

"May I?" Patsy asks, and I nod.

"I'll put the kettle on. Is that apple pie in the bag?" I take the shopping bag from her, and take a snoop, discovering the warm bake, before she tells me to please go ahead and cut the pie.

We sit in a companionable silence over mugs of tea and the aromas of cinnamon and nutmeg wafting from our plates of pie and custard.

"I'm so glad you brought the custard," I tell her, shoving a heaped spoon into my mouth. Apparently, I was really hungry, but didn't realise it until Patsy arrived with fresh confectionery.

"Adam would have a fit if he knew I was living off tea and biscuits," I confide in her. "He's always been a bit of a three-veg-and-meat guy, staying far away from sweets. Except for Mum's shortbread—that's always been his weakness."

Patsy smiles, but her eyes cloud over, and I put my spoon down. "I'm sorry, did I say–?"

"No, no. Not at all. I've just missed him so much... I'm his mother and I don't even know what his favourite food is." Her hands are shaking as she picks up the mug and takes a sip to control her emotions. I put a hand on her arm and give it a squeeze.

"I wanted to show you something," she says, reaching for her handbag before handing me a very old photo. It's faded with age and the corners are worn from handling. I immediately recognise a young Patsy, cheeks still full with youth and long hair cascading over her shoulders, but she's not looking directly at the camera, she's looking at the baby in her arms. A tiny, squished face is the only part that's visible and poking out of the cocoon of blankets.

I look at her and she nods.

"It's the only photo I have of Adam when he was born. I snuck a camera, I borrowed from a friend, into the maternity ward and asked a nurse to take the photo for me. It was only weeks later that Robert had enough money saved, from caddying on the weekends, for us to have the film developed."

"You kept it all this time," I say softly, worried that even a gentle word will break the woman in front of me. She's beautiful and brittle and filled to the brim with regret.

"I know Adam doesn't have many photos of his child-hood...so I wanted to give it to you, to keep for him."

"We'll make a copy," I say immediately and she readily agrees.

"Stella looks just like him," I say, studying the image a bit more, and we both agree that there's a resemblance in the Cupid's-bow lips.

Patsy insists on staying to cook me dinner, and I don't protest this time. I get it now that she needs to feel useful, to make up for all the years she missed. And to be perfectly honest, a meal that hasn't come out of a foil container sounds wonderful. It gives me some time to sit and feed Stella without the nagging in my head that there's still food to be cooked and laundry to be done. I nurse my daughter, studying every inch of her little face with the same awe I do every day. But today I also have the photo of Adam as a baby in my head, and a rush of love for Stella, Adam, and our future life in this cottage, that means so much to us, and which he basically rebuilt with his own hands, floods me. God, I miss him.

Delicious smells from the kitchen—fried mushrooms for stroganoff—make my mouth water as I hold Stella to my breast for the early evening feed. It's then that the phone rings. No number means it's either someone trying to sell me insurance or it's Adam phoning from the satellite phone. But it can't be Adam; he called me just the other day, and calls are spaced two weeks apart. I answer, and end up pressing the phone to my ear with my shoulder as I reposition Stella who has dozed off in my arms.

"Evie? Can you hear me?"

My heart stops. In an instant, I'm equally elated and terrified. He should not be calling me. He sounds so far away. He's on the other side of the world while I'm so close to the vital parts of him: his mother and daughter. This realisation seems to amplify my angst, but I try to keep my emotions in check because the last thing a soldier needs is a wife who's falling apart without him.

"I can hear you!" I say loudly.

"Oh, darling it's so good to hear your voice." He sounds tired.

"Adam, is everything okay?" I find myself sitting up

straighter and I'm aware of Patsy, hovering between the kitchen and living room. I listen. He doesn't have much time to talk. The last thing he says is that he loves me before we're cut off by a poor connection.

"Was that Adam?" Patsy is drying her hands on a tea towel as she comes to sit beside me on the sofa.

I nod.

"Evie, what's the matter?"

There's no easy way to tell a mother bad news about her child, so I take a deep breath and tell her.

"Adam's been badly injured. He's coming home."

ADAM

I LAND at Heathrow two months too soon. Just behind the tinted doors, separating passengers from the family and friends who come to greet them, waits my family.

The third-degree burns on my left arm and leg make me useless for active duty. Fortunately, my fingers were spared, and for that I am grateful. I shouldered my way into the fire to haul MacGill out. It's a mystery to everyone, including me, how I managed to lug him to safety. His ankle broke in two places when he tripped. If the squad hadn't arrived with the extinguishers when they did, the Scott and I would be toast. Quite literally.

I carry my bag in my good hand and search the crowd for Evie. She has tied a red balloon to Stella's arm, and the balloon bobs above the sea of heads. I drop my bag and collide with Evie, Stella strapped to her in a kangaroo pouch. I kiss them both, again and again.

"You're home," Evie whispers, cupping my face in her hands, kissing me again. She tastes of tea and home.

"I am." I smile through the kisses.

I know it's a cliché, but I can't believe how much Stella has grown. Her face has changed so much, revealing a clearer blend of Evie and me.

Evie looks at my arm, heavily bandaged. She swallows her tears and narrows her eyes. "How soon can they do the first skin graft?"

"In a few months. Depends on how quickly I start healing."

"And the pain?"

"Manageable...mostly."

"Therapy?" She interrogates me like only she can, always shoving me in the direction I need to be, whether I realise it or not.

"Yes, more therapy. No man wants to be having dreams about that Scotsman, believe me," I joke.

She slaps me on the chest, her palm connecting with the ring in my pocket. She looks up at me, eyes wide with curiosity. "What's that?"

"Nothing," I say sheepishly. While the inner workings of Evie's mind still often elude me, today I see hope, followed by suspicion in her green eyes. She tries to remove her hand, but I stop her, and keep her palm there, sheltering my heart. And then, in the middle of the comings and goings of the airport, I drop down on one knee. I lift her hand and kiss it, before I loosen the button of the pocket with my healthy hand, and take out the ring.

I see Evie register what's about to happen. She covers her face with her hands in astonishment. I wait. When she wipes her tears away, I say the words I've been rehearsing for seven hours straight in the plane.

"Like this ring, we've been through a ring of fire of our own and come out the other side. Not unscathed, but stronger. I don't want to imagine my life without you and Stella. You are my whole world. I love you. You make me a better man, Evie. Will you marry me?"

Evie nods. "Yes. Yes!"

The crowd that has formed around us cheers. I slip the ring on Evie's finger and bring her face to mine.

"You, it's always been you," I tell her.

TWENTY-TWO

ADAM

"Suffering has been stronger than all other teaching, and has taught me to understand what your heart used to be. I have been bent and broken, but—I hope—into a better shape."

I READ these words over again. Today they resonate hard. My heart is full. Stella and I are lying on a blanket under the oak tree, with Fosters assuming her usual position as close protection to her baby. She lifts her head when she sees Evie approach with a wooden board laden with cheese, fruit, and bread. It was Evie's idea to make the most of the good weather and take lunch in our garden today.

My wife—how I love the sound of that—joins me on the blanket, and our daughter, now almost nine months old, has rolled over onto her belly and pushed herself up on all fours, rocking back and forth, raring to go to all the places her dimpled knees and chubby hands will take her.

"She's a little firecracker, isn't she?" I say.

"Mmm," Evie pretends to be unimpressed, but the slight upturn of her lips tells a different story. She has fully come into her own as a mother, already finding creative ways to balance her art and taking care of Stella when I'm working away on film sets with my brother.

Evie reaches for Fosters, and I see her brow furrow with concern.

"What's the matter?" I ask.

Evie leans closer to Fosters, her hand gently kneading her soft underbelly, then she brushes the fur back against the grain of its growth.

"Adam, is it possible that Fosters could be pregnant?"

I shake my head. "Unlikely. Army dogs are usually neutered."

"But her nipples are so engorged, and look, her belly looks...heavy."

I scoot over to inspect her, and Evie is right. Fosters is showing all the signs of pregnancy.

"But how could it have even happened?" I ask Evie who raises an eyebrow as if to ask me if I've suddenly gone daft.

"Do you think it happened that time we left the gate open and she went on a walkabout for half an hour?" Evie suggests.

I recall it—it was about two months ago, and actually she had taken herself for a walk up the lane on the Saturday and the Sunday, and then came back when my work was done and I called her. I didn't think anything of it; Fosters was well known to our neighbours and I knew she wouldn't go far.

It seems to dawn on Evie and me at the same time that there were only two possibilities in close proximity for the sire.

"Boxer!" I exclaim, referring to Donny and Sue's down-the-lane Boxer named Boxer.

"Or, Amik," Evie reminds me of the beautiful, but rather vicious Chow Chow in the other direction.

We both start laughing when we imagine what the cross-breed pups will look like, and I tell Evie I will call for an appointment at the vet in the village later.

WHEN IT'S CONFIRMED that Fosters is indeed expecting and probably just days away from giving birth, we decide to throw her a puppy shower in the garden, inviting our close-knit family and friends to join us in the celebration. We also invite Don, Sue, and Boxer, and Lydia who owns Milo.

While I stand at the barbecue, turning burgers, sausages, and kebabs, I look up to see that my life is full and bursting with people who love me. Meeting Evie, and becoming Stella's dad, pried open my broken, stubborn, scared heart and healed it from the inside.

Evie wraps her arms around me from behind and gives me a squeeze.

"Hello, husband," she says.

"Hello, wife," I say, smiling even though I know she can't see my face.

"What are you so deep in thought about?" she asks.

"Sausages," I joke.

She slaps me with an open palm on the arse, and I pretend that it actually hurt.

"Actually," I say, setting the tongs down, and pulling her close, "I was thinking of how damn lucky I am. Look around us, Evie. All these people..."

"Came for a puppy shower. Ridiculous, right?" she teases and I shut her up with a deep kiss that goes on long enough for Leo and Robby to wolf-whistle from the other end of the garden, inviting everyone there to watch us kiss. But I don't care. This moment...my life is perfect.

THE END.

AFTERWORD

I blame my fascination with all things military on my husband, Grant, but it was a single paragraph in Kim Hughes' military biography, *Painting the Sand* (*Simon & Schuster,* 2018) that inspired Adam and Evie's story. I'd read a few other biographies about ex- special forces soldiers, but Kim Hughes' account of being an explosives' expert for the British Army planted a seed in my imagination that took root. I have to wonder how he would feel knowing his work inspired a romance novel?!

Thank you Mr Hughes. Your story stuck with me.

ACKNOWLEDGMENTS

They say it takes a village to raise a child. I think the same is true for bringing a book into the world. Even when you are "self-publishing" it's by no means a one woman show, so bear with me as I say thank you to all the people who helped, encouraged and inspired me while I wrote and got *Trust Me* ready for publication.

Thank you to the regular attendees of the Sutton Writers workshop: Kirsteen, Jonathan, Paul, Matthew, Sarah, Claudia and Matt G, who read bits and pieces and wonky first drafts and offered loads of encouragement and gave me excellent feedback.

My accountability group: Lauren, Sarah and Matthew who keep me chasing word counts to get the draft done and then helped me face the edits and revisions and generally cheered me on through the process. You guys rock!

Jonathan, thank you for reading and rereading and being a brilliant sound board and indie advocate while I've been getting the book reading for publication. Having someone to figure out the 'what next' on the indie publishing journey has made all the difference.

Juanine, it didn't matter how many times I asked you read stuff over and over again, you never minded and always gave me honest feedback. Thank you.

My girls, Juanine, Nancy, Lee and Monique, Bridget, Yvette, Kim, Lucy, Charlene, Crystle-Lynne thank you for always showing up for my live reviews and cheering me on.

Kim, you are always one of my first readers. Your feedback always means so much me. Thank you for telling me from the get go that you loved it. It made me believe in myself.

Caroline, you cheered me on all the way. Thank you.

My sister, Brenda. You gushed and gushed about this book. Thank you, sis!

My mom, Esther. Thank you teaching me how to read at an early age and for encouraging it by taking me to the library and letting me read whatever I wanted (mostly Danielle Steel, haha!). You're my biggest fan, and that makes me so happy.

My husband, Grant. ♡ You moved your office into the basement so that I could have a space of my own to write. That in itself was a dream come true for me. Thank you for always, always giving all the time and space I've needed to explore my passion and creative self. You love me more:-)

Editing: Katherine Bosman. Thank you for helping me revise, fix and layer Adam and Evie's story.

Proofreading: Juanine Grutzner. Thank you for the final polish.

Cover design: Tallulah Habib. It was s such a chore looking through all those bare chested models, but we managed didn't we? Ha! Thank you for doing your magic with the cover yet again.

Without these extraordinary and talented individuals *Trust Me* might never have come to be.

ABOUT THE AUTHOR

Cindi Page writes about second chances in love because she got one of her own when she was reunited with her high school sweetheart after more than a decade of living on opposite ends of the world. Originally from South Africa, she now lives in London with her husband, two sons and her Shihtzu princess, Charlie.

Trust Me is her third indie novel, a military-inspired romance.

Find her on her favourite social platform as @cindirellawrites

Printed in Great Britain
by Amazon